THE BALLAD OF BLACK TOM

VICTOR LAVALLE

A TOM DOHERTY ASSOCIATES BOOK

NEW YORK

This is a work of fiction. All of the characters, organizations, and events portrayed in this novella are either products of the author's imagination or are used fictitiously.

THE BALLAD OF BLACK TOM

Copyright © 2016 by Victor LaValle
Cover art by Robert Hunt
Edited by Ellen Datlow

A Tor.com Book
Published by Tom Doherty Associates, LLC
175 Fifth Avenue
New York, NY 10010

www.tor.com

Tor® is a registered trademark of Tom Doherty Associates, LLC.

ISBN 978-0-7653-8661-8 (e-book)
ISBN 978-0-7653-8786-8 (trade paperback)

First Edition: February 2016

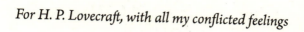

For H. P. Lovecraft, with all my conflicted feelings

PART 1

TOMMY TESTER

1

PEOPLE WHO MOVE TO NEW YORK always make the same mistake. They can't see the place. This is true of Manhattan, but even the outer boroughs, too, be it Flushing Meadows in Queens or Red Hook in Brooklyn. They come looking for magic, whether evil or good, and nothing will convince them it isn't here. This wasn't all bad, though. Some New Yorkers had learned how to make a living from this error in thinking. Charles Thomas Tester for one.

The morning of most importance began with a trip from Charles's apartment in Harlem. He'd been hired to make a delivery to a house out in Queens. He shared the crib in Harlem with his ailing father, Otis, a man who'd been dying ever since his wife of twenty-one years expired. They'd had one child, Charles Thomas, and even though he was twenty and exactly the age for independence, he played the role of dutiful son. Charles worked to support his dying dad. He hustled to provide food and shelter and a little extra to lay on a number from time to time. God knows he didn't make any more than that.

A little after 8:00 a.m., he left the apartment in his gray flannel suit; the slacks were cuffed but scuffed and the sleeves conspicuously short. Fine fabric, but frayed. This gave Charles a certain look. Like a gentleman without a gentleman's bank account. He picked the brown leather brogues with nicked toes. Then the seal-brown trooper hat instead of the fedora. The trooper hat's brim showed its age and wear, and this was good for his hustle, too. Last, he took the guitar case, essential to complete the look. He left the guitar itself at home with his bedridden father. Inside he carried only a yellow book, not much larger than a pack of cards.

As Charles Thomas Tester left the apartment on West 144th Street, he heard his father plucking at the strings in the back bedroom. The old man could spend half a day playing that instrument and singing along to the radio at his bedside. Charles expected to be back home before midday, his guitar case empty and his wallet full.

"Who's that writing?" his father sang, voice hoarse but the more lovely for it. "I said who's that writing?"

Before leaving, Charles sang back the last line of the chorus. "John the Revelator." He was embarrassed by his voice, not tuneful at all, at least when compared with his dad's.

In the apartment Charles Thomas Tester went by Charles, but on the street everyone knew him as Tommy.

Tommy Tester, always carrying a guitar case. This wasn't because he aspired to be a musician; in fact he could barely remember a handful of songs and his singing voice might be described, kindly, as wobbly. His father, who'd made a living as a bricklayer, and his mother, who'd spent her life working as a domestic, had loved music. Dad played guitar and Mother could really stroll on a piano. It was only natural that Tommy Tester ended up drawn to performing, the only tragedy being that he lacked talent. He thought of himself as an entertainer. There were others who would have called him a scammer, a swindler, a con, but he never thought of himself this way. No good charlatan ever did.

In the clothes he'd picked, he sure looked the part of the dazzling, down-and-out musician. He was a man who drew notice and enjoyed it. He walked to the train station as if he were on his way to play a rent party alongside Willie "The Lion" Smith. And Tommy had played with Willie's band once. After a single song Willie threw Tommy out. And yet Tommy toted that guitar case like the businessmen proudly carrying their briefcases off to work now. The streets of Harlem had gone haywire in 1924, with blacks arriving from the South and the West Indies. A crowded part of the city found itself with more folks to accommodate. Tommy Tester enjoyed all this just fine. Walking through Harlem first thing in the morning was like being a single drop of blood inside an enormous body that was waking up. Brick and mortar, elevated train tracks, and miles of underground pipe, this city lived; day and night it thrived.

Tommy took up more room than most because of the guitar case. At the 143rd Street entrance he had to lift the case over his head while climbing the stairs to the elevated track. The little yellow book inside thumped but didn't weigh much. He rode all the way down to 57th Street and there transferred for the Roosevelt Avenue Corona Line of the BMT. It was his second time going out to Queens, the first being when he'd taken the special job that would be completed today.

The farther Tommy Tester rode into Queens the more conspicuous he became. Far fewer Negroes lived in Flushing than in Harlem. Tommy bumped his hat slightly lower on his head. The conductor entered the car twice, and both times he stopped to make conversation with Tommy. Once to ask if he was a musician, knocking the guitar case as if it were his own, and the second time to ask if Tommy had missed his stop. The other passengers feigned disinterest even as Tommy saw them listening for his replies. Tommy kept the answers simple: "Yes, sir, I play guitar" and "No, sir, got a couple more stops still." Becoming unremarkable, invisible, compliant—these were useful tricks for a black man in an all-white neighborhood. Survival techniques. At the last stop, Main Street, Tommy Tester got off with all the others—Irish and German immigrants mostly—and made his way down to street level. A long walk from here.

The whole way Tommy marveled at the broad streets and garden apartments. Though the borough had grown, modernized greatly since its former days as Dutch and British farmland, to a boy like Tommy, raised in Harlem, all this appeared rustic and bewilderingly open. The open arms of the natural world worried him as much as the white people, both so alien to him. When he passed whites on the street, he kept his gaze down and his shoulders soft. Men from Harlem were known for their strut, a lion's stride, but out here he hid it away. He was surveyed but never stopped. His foot-shuffling disguise held up fine. And finally, amid the blocks and blocks of newly built garden apartments, Tommy Tester found his destination.

A private home, small and nearly lost in a copse of trees, the rest of the block taken up by a mortuary. The private place grew like a tumor on the house of the dead. Tommy Tester turned up the walkway and didn't even have to knock. Before he'd climbed the three steps, the front door cracked open. A tall, gaunt woman stood in the doorway, half in shadows. Ma Att. That was the name he had for her, the only one she answered to. She'd hired him like this. On this doorstep, through a half-open door. Word had traveled to Harlem that she needed help and he was the type of man who could acquire what she needed. Summoned to her door and given a job without being invited in. The same would happen now. He understood, or could at least guess, at the reason. What would the neighbors say if this woman had Negroes coming freely into her home?

Tommy undid the latch of the guitar case and held it open. Ma Att leaned forward so her head peeked out into the daylight. Inside lay the book, no larger than the palm of Tommy's hand. Its front and back covers were sallow yellow. Three words had been etched on both sides. *Zig Zag Zig.* Tommy didn't know what the words meant, nor did he care to know. He hadn't read this book, never even touched it with his bare hands. He'd been hired to transport the little yellow book, and that was all he'd done. He'd been the right man for this task, in part, because he knew he shouldn't do any more than that. A good hustler isn't curious. A good hustler only wants his pay.

Ma Att looked from the book, there in the case, and back to him. She seemed slightly disappointed.

"You weren't tempted to look inside?" she asked.

"I charge more for that," Tommy said.

She didn't find him funny. She sniffled once, that's all. Then she reached into the guitar case and slipped the book out. She moved so quickly the book hardly had a chance to catch even a single ray of sunlight, but still, as the book was pulled into the darkness of Ma Att's home, a faint trail of smoke appeared in the air. Even glancing contact with daylight had set the book on fire. She slapped at the cover once, snuffing out the spark.

"Where did you find it?" she asked.

"There's a place in Harlem," Tommy said, his voice hushed. "It's called the Victoria Society. Even the hardest gangsters in Harlem are afraid to go there. It's where people like me trade in books like yours. And worse."

Here he stopped. Mystery lingered in the air like the scent of scorched book. Ma Att actually leaned forward as if he'd landed a hook into her lip. But Tommy said no more.

"The Victoria Society," she whispered. "How much would you charge to take me in?"

Tommy scanned the old woman's face. How much might she pay? He wondered at the sum, but still he shook his head. "I'd feel terrible if you got hurt in there. I'm sorry."

Ma Att watched Tommy Tester, calculating how bad a place this Victoria Society could be. After all, a person who trafficked in books like the little yellow one in her hand was hardly the frail kind.

Ma Att reached out and tapped the mailbox, affixed

to the outside wall, with one finger. Tommy opened it to find his pay. Two hundred dollars. He counted through the cash right there, in front of her. Enough for six months' rent, utilities, food and all.

"You shouldn't be in this neighborhood when the sun goes down," Ma Att said. She didn't sound concerned for him.

"I'll be back in Harlem before lunchtime. I wouldn't suggest you visit there, day or night." He tipped his cap, snapped the empty guitar case shut, and turned away from Ma Att's door.

On the way back to the train, Tommy Tester decided to find his friend Buckeye. Buckeye worked for Madame St. Clair, the numbers queen of Harlem. Tommy should play Ma Att's address tonight. If his number came up, he'd have enough to buy himself a better guitar case. Maybe even his own guitar.

2

"THAT'S A FINE GIT-FIDDLE."

Tommy Tester didn't even have to look up to know he'd found a new mark. He simply had to see the quality of the man's shoes, the bottom end of a fine cane. He plucked at his guitar, still getting used to the feel of the new instrument, and hummed instead of sang because he sounded more like a talented musician when he didn't open his mouth.

The trip out to Queens last month had inspired Tommy Tester to travel more. The streets of Harlem could get pretty crowded with singers and guitar players, men on brass instruments, and every one of them put his little operation to shame. Where Tommy had three songs in his catalog, each of those men had thirty, three hundred. But on the way home from Ma Att's place, he'd realized he hadn't passed a single strummer along the way. The singer on the street might've been more common in Harlem and down in Five Points, or more modern parts of Brooklyn, but so much of this city remained—essentially—a bit of jumped-up countryside.

None of the other Harlem players would take a train out to Queens or rural Brooklyn for the chance of getting money from the famously thrifty immigrants homesteading in those parts. But a man like Tommy Tester—who only put on a show of making music—certainly might. Those outer-borough bohunks and Paddys probably didn't know a damn thing about serious jazz, so Tommy's knockoff version might still stand out.

On returning from Ma Att's place, he'd talked all this through with his father. Otis Tester, yet one more time, offered to get him work as a bricklayer, join the profession. A kind gesture, a loving father's attempt, but not one that worked on his son. Tommy Tester would never say it out loud—it'd hurt the old man too much—but working construction had given his father gnarled hands and a stooped back, nothing more. Otis Tester had earned a Negro's wage, not a white man's, as was common in 1924, and even that money was withheld if the foreman sometimes wanted a bit more in his pocket. What was a Negro going to do? Complain to whom? There was a union, but Negroes weren't allowed to join. Less money and erratic pay *were* the job. Just as surely as mixing the mortar when laborers didn't show up to do it. The companies that'd hired Otis Tester, that'd always assured him he was one of them, had filled his job the same day his body finally broke down. Otis, a proud man, had tried to instill a sense of duty in his only child, as had Tommy's mother. But the lesson Tommy Tester learned instead was that you better have a way to make your own money because this world wasn't trying to make a Negro rich. As long as Tommy paid their rent and brought home food, how could his father complain? When he played Ma Att's number, it hit as he dreamed it would, and he bought a fine guitar and case. Now it was common for Tommy and Otis to spend their evenings playing harmonies well into the night. Tommy had even become moderately better with a tune.

Tommy had decided against a return to Flushing, Queens, though. A hustler's premonition told him he didn't want to run into Ma Att again. After all, the book he'd given her had been missing one page, hadn't it? The very last page. Tommy Tester had done this with purpose. It rendered the tome useless, harmless. He'd done this because he knew exactly what he'd been hired to deliver. The Supreme Alphabet. He didn't have to read through it to be aware of its power. Tommy doubted very much the old woman wanted the little yellow book for casual reading. He hadn't touched the book with his bare hands and hadn't read a single word inside, but there were still ways to get the last sheet of parchment free safely. In fact that page remained in Tommy's apartment, folded into a square, slipped right inside the body of the old guitar he always left with his father. Tommy had been warned not to read the pages, and he'd kept to that rule. His father had been the one to tear out the last sheet, and his father could not read. His illiteracy served as a safeguard. This is how you hustle the arcane. Skirt the rules but don't break them.

Today Tommy Tester had come to the Reformed Church in Flatbush, Brooklyn; as far from home as Flushing, and lacking an angry sorceress. He wore the same outfit as when he went to visit Ma Att, his trooper hat upside down at his feet. He'd set himself up in front of the church's iron-railed graveyard. A bit of theater in this choice, but the right kind of person would be drawn to this picture. The black jazz man in his frayed dignity singing softly at the burying ground.

Tommy Tester knew two jazz songs and one bit of blues. He played the blues tune for two hours because it sounded more somber. He didn't bother with the words any longer, only the chords and a humming accompaniment. And then the old man with the fine shoes and the cane appeared. He listened quietly for a time before he spoke.

"That's a fine git-fiddle," the man finally said.

And it was the term—*git-fiddle*—that assured Tommy his hustle had worked. As simple as that. The old man wanted Tommy to know he could speak the language. Tommy played a few more chords and ended without flourish. Finally he looked up to find the older man flushed, grinning. The man was round and short, and his hair blew out wildly like a dandelion's soft white blowball. His beard was coming in, bristly and gray. He didn't look like a wealthy man, but it was the well-off who could afford such a disguise. You had to be rich to risk looking broke. The shoes verified the man's wealth, though. And his cane, with a handle shaped like an animal head, cast in what looked like pure gold.

"My name is Robert Suydam," the man said. Then waited, as if the name alone should make Tommy Tester bow. "I am having a party at my home. You will play for my guests. Such dusky tunes will suit the mood."

"You want me to sing?" Tommy asked. "You want to pay me to sing?"

"Come to my home in three nights."

Robert Suydam pointed toward Martense Street. The old man lived there in a mansion hidden within a disorder of trees. He promised Tommy five hundred dollars for the job. Otis Tester had never made more than nine hundred in a year. Suydam took out a billfold and handed Tommy one hundred dollars. All ten-dollar bills.

"A retainer," Suydam said.

Tommy set the guitar flat in its case and accepted the bills, turning them over. 1923 bills. Andrew Jackson appeared on the front. The image of Old Hickory didn't look directly at Tommy, but glanced aside as if catching sight of something just over Tommy Tester's right shoulder.

"When you arrive at the house, you must say one word and only this word to gain entrance."

Tommy stopped counting the money, folded it over twice, and slipped it into the inner pocket of his jacket.

"I can't promise what will happen if you forget it," Suydam said, then paused to watch Tommy, assessing him.

"Ashmodai," Suydam said. "That is the word. Let me hear you say it."

"Ashmodai," Tommy repeated.

Robert Suydam tapped the cane on the pavement twice and walked away. Tommy watched him go for three blocks before he picked up his hat and put it on. He clicked the guitar case shut. But before Tommy Tester took even one step toward the train station, he got gripped, hard, on the back of the neck.

Two white men appeared. One was tall and thin, the other tall and wide. Together they resembled the number *10*. The wide one kept his hand on Tommy's neck. He knew this one was a cop, or had been once. Up in Harlem they called this grip John's Handshake. The thin one stayed two paces back.

The surprise of it all caused Tommy to forget the pose of deference he'd normally adopt when cops stopped him. Instead he acted like himself, his father's son, a kid from Harlem, a proud man who didn't take kindly to being given shit.

"You're coming on a little strong," he told the wide one.

"And you're far from home," the wide one replied.

"You don't know where I live," Tommy snapped back.

The wide one reached into Tommy's coat and removed the ten-dollar bills. "We saw you take these from the old man," he began. "That old man is part of an ongoing investigation, so this is evidence."

He slipped the bills into his slacks and watched Tommy to gauge his reaction.

"Police business," Tommy said coolly, and stopped thinking that the money had ever been his.

The wide one pointed at the thin one. "He's police. I'm private."

Tommy looked from the private detective to the cop. Tall and thin and lantern-jawed, his eyes dispassionate and surveying. "Malone," he finally offered. "And this is . . ."

The wide one cut him off. "He doesn't need my name. He didn't need yours, either."

Malone looked exasperated. This strong-arm routine

didn't seem like his style. Tommy Tester read both men quickly. The private detective had the bearing of a brute while the other one, Malone, appeared too sensitive for a cop's job. Tommy considered that he'd stayed a few paces back to keep away from the private dick, not Tommy.

"What's your business with Mr. Suydam?" the private detective asked. He pulled Tommy's hat off and looked inside as if there might be more money.

"He liked my music," Tommy said. Then, calm enough now to remember the situation, he added another word quickly. "Sir."

"I heard your voice," the private detective said. "Nobody could enjoy that."

Tommy Tester would've liked to argue the point, but even a corrupt, violent brute could be right sometimes. Robert Suydam wasn't paying five hundred dollars for Tommy's voice. For what, then?

"Now me and Detective Malone are going to keep strolling with Mr. Suydam, keeping him safe. And you're going to go back home, isn't that right? Where's home?"

"Harlem," Tommy offered. "Sir."

"Of course it is," Malone said quietly.

"Home to Harlem, then," the private detective added. He set the hat back on Tommy's head and gave Malone a quick, derisive glance. He turned in the direction where the old man had gone, and only then did Malone step any closer to Tommy. Standing this near, Tommy could sense a kind of sadness in the gaunt officer. His eyes suggested a man disappointed with the world.

Tommy waited before reaching down for his guitar case. No sudden moves in front of even a sullen cop. Just because Malone wasn't as rough as the private detective didn't mean he was gentle.

"Why did he give you that money?" Malone asked. "Why really?"

He asked, but seemed to doubt an honest answer would come. Instead there was a set to his lips, and a narrowness in his gaze, that suggested he was probing for an answer to some other question. Tommy worried he'd mention the performance at Suydam's home in three nights. If they weren't happy about Tommy talking with Suydam on the street, how would they act upon learning he planned to visit the old man's home? Tommy lost one hundred dollars to the private detective, but he was damned if he'd give up the promise of four hundred dollars more. He decided to play a role that always worked on whites. The Clueless Negro.

"I cain't says, suh," Tommy began. "I's just a simple geetar man."

Malone came close to smiling for the first time. "You're not simple," he said.

Tommy watched Malone walk off to catch up with

the private detective. He looked over his shoulder. "And you're right to stay out of Queens," Malone said. "That old woman isn't happy with what you did to her book!"

Malone walked off and Tommy Tester remained there, feeling exposed—*seen*—in a way he'd never experienced.

"You're a cop," Tommy called. "Can't you protect me?"

Malone looked back once more. "Guns and badges don't scare everyone."

3

TOMMY'S BEST FRIEND, BUCKEYE, arrived in Harlem
in 1920 when he was sixteen years old. At fourteen he'd
left the tiny Caribbean island of Montserrat to work on
the Panama Canal, and from Panama made his way to
the United States, to Harlem. He arrived expecting to
do the same work as he'd done on the
canal—construction—but soon found out what Otis
Tester had long known: Negroes had no protection.
Buckeye broke an ankle at the age of seventeen and
found himself out of day labor for two months. When he
was ready to return, the job had been filled, and besides
that, the ankle never healed well. He couldn't be on it
for long hours, couldn't tote much weight without it giving out. Soon he found his way to Madame St. Clair and
her famous numbers game. She hired him because she
needed men from the Caribbean, who knew and would
be trusted by the recent West Indian immigrants.
Madame St. Clair evolved in changing times, and because of this she thrived. The regular kickbacks to local
police also helped. Buckeye met Tommy Tester in this

milieu. Tommy played a club where Buckeye made business. One evening Buckeye sidled next to Tommy at the bar and asked where he'd learned to sing so badly. Did he take lessons or was it a natural gift? They became fast friends.

Now Tommy Tester led his father out of their building and down the block. He'd returned home from the encounter with Robert Suydam, with Malone and the private detective, and felt himself in need of a night out. It took time to convince Otis to step out. Otis never left the apartment, hardly left his bedroom. He'd become like a dog gone into the dark so he could die alone, but Tommy had different plans. Or maybe he needed his father too much to let him go easily.

Buckeye left an open invitation for Tommy at the Victoria Society. It was on 137th Street. The walk was a mere seven blocks, but because of his father's health, it took them half an hour to arrive.

The Victoria Society consisted of three modest rooms on the second floor of an apartment building. It was a Caribbean social club. Down on the street Tommy and Otis were in black Harlem; in the Victoria Society they entered the British West Indies. The flags of every Caribbean nation were fixed to the walls of a long hallway. A much larger Union Jack hung at the far end. At the doorway to the warren of rooms, Tommy Tester had to give Buckeye's name three times. The greeter at the door remained unmoved until Tommy used Buckeye's given name, George Hurley. That worked like a spell.

Tommy and Otis followed the greeter at a distance. One of the society's rooms was reserved for men playing card games or bones; the second showed men in lounge chairs smoking and listening to music played at a respectable volume; and the third had card tables set out with tablecloths and chairs, for meals. Buckeye had invited Tommy to the Victoria Society many times in the years since they'd made friends, but Tommy had never come until now. He felt a sting, like a slap, across his face. This was the place he'd described to Ma Att? The shorthand for a den of crime and sin? The place where Harlem's worst criminals were too afraid to go?

He'd assumed he knew what kind of place this would be. Buckeye ran numbers for the most famous female gangster in New York City, so why wouldn't the Victoria Society be like those legendary opium dens? Or had Tommy simply assumed terrible things about this wave of West Indian immigrants? The American Negroes in Harlem got up to awful gossip about those newcomers. And now he'd come to find the Victoria Society might as well be a British tearoom. He felt slightly disappointed. He'd brought his father because he'd meant to show his dad a scandalous night. He'd heard women danced in nearly nothing, so close they practically sat in your lap. Being inside now, seeing this place truly, was like learning another world existed within—or alongside—the world he'd always known. Worse, all this time he'd been too ignorant to realize it. The idea troubled him like a pinched nerve.

Tommy and his dad sat, and the older man blew out a deep breath. Otis spent a long time adjusting himself in the chair to minimize his back pain. He moved like someone ancient. Otis Tester was forty-one years old.

A thin woman came to the table offering dinner she'd made in her kitchen, then brought here to sell. She was Trinidadian. Her dinner plates were already prepared, and she rolled them through the dining room on a cart. Saheena, pineapple chow, and macaroni pie. A bowl of cow heel soup. Tall cups of passion fruit juice. The whole meal, for both men, came to a dollar. Tommy paid.

"I don't know what any of this mess is," Otis said, watching the plate in front of him like it might strike. "Why didn't we go down to Bo's place?"

Tommy found himself watching the Trinidadian woman because she reminded him of his own mother. That wiry frame and splay-footed walk. Irene Tester, gone four years now. People who knew her well used to call her Michigan because she never could stop talking about the place where her parents came from. She collapsed on a bus, died thirty-seven years old among strangers. Life as a domestic wore her out just as surely as construction did Otis. Tommy looked to his father, wondering if he'd also been thinking the Trinidadian woman looked like Irene, but the old man only stared down at the plates, mystified.

"Come on, now," Tommy said. "There's something here you're going to like."

Otis scanned the table looking for something he recognized. He lifted a fork and poked at the macaroni pie. "This is just cheese and noodles, yes?"

Tommy Tester sank a fork and knife into his serving. He brought a portion to his mouth and chewed. After swallowing, he nodded, but his father prodded at it anyway, as if he didn't trust his son. He set the fork down without eating.

"Now, you say this white man is going to pay you how much?"

"Four hundred dollars."

"All that just to play at his party?" Otis asked. He grabbed the cup of passion fruit juice, brought it to his nose, sniffed, set the drink back down. "All that for *you* to play at his party?"

Tommy chewed at a bite of the pineapple chow. It was sweet, but the kick of lime juice and hot pepper followed soon after. He gulped his juice to cool his throat.

"That's what he said."

Otis raised his hands in the air, held them as far apart as he could.

"That's the distance between what a white man says to a Negro and what he really means."

Tommy knew this, of course. Hadn't he lived twenty years in America already? His whole hustle—*entertainment*—was predicated on the idea that people had ulterior motives for hiring him.

When he dressed in those frayed clothes and played at the blues man or the jazz man or even the docile Negro, he knew the role bestowed a kind of power upon him. Give people what they expect and you can take from them all that you need. They won't realize you've juiced them until they're dry. Ma Att had essentially paid him to deliver a worthless item, hadn't she? If he had to play the role of quasi-gangster to get paid, then so be it. He played the roles needed to enrich his bank account. But all this would sound criminal to Otis. Or demeaning. The man had an outsized opinion of dignity. Nobility didn't pay well enough to make Tommy want the job.

"I'll be real careful, Daddy."

Otis Tester watched his son quietly. The rest of the dining room grew louder as more tables filled, but a kind of quiet, a bubble of reserve, surrounded their table. Otis was father to a twenty-year-old black boy who'd blithely explained he'd be going out to Flatbush, in the middle of the night, into the home of a white man. He might as well have told his father he planned to go wrestle a bear.

"When I left Oklahoma City," Otis Tester said, "I rode on the railroads. Hobo'd all the way east."

Not the first time, nor the five-hundredth time, Tommy Tester had heard this story. Tommy ate to keep from expressing his disappointment. Hadn't Otis heard the most vital detail? *Four hundred dollars.*

"I avoided crossing Arkansas," Otis continued. "Whether you were Negro, white, or a red man they were pretty rough on hoboing in Arkansas. They had chain gangs, you know. I went to East St. Louis, over to Evansville. I got taken off the train once in Decatur. I wasn't making a direct route here. I was real young so I had the need to see much more than my final destination."

Finally Otis Tester ate the macaroni pie, as if storytelling had sparked his appetite. He took one bite, chewed cautiously, but after he swallowed the first, he chomped down two more.

"Like I said, they took me off the train in Decatur. And that's when it turned out I had to use my head." Now he took the risk of a drink. The passion fruit juice clearly pleased him. He sipped slowly, then set the drink down. "I had to use this."

Otis Tester unbuttoned the top two buttons of his

shirt right there in the dining room. Tommy stiffened, feeling like a five-year-old whose daddy was about to shame him in public. But before he could scold his father, or reach over and try to cover Otis's exposed skin, the old man pulled something from around his neck. It was hanging there on a coarse string. He slipped it off and clutched it in one rough hand while he buttoned his shirt again. Tommy leaned forward trying to see what his dad held. Otis Tester extended his hand, opened it.

A straight razor lay in his palm.

"I carried this with me the whole time I rode the trains," Otis said. "White man, Negro, or Red Indian was not going to get an easy shot at me."

He knocked one end of the razor on the table loudly.

"In Decatur, I made some people understand this," Otis said.

Tommy looked from the razor to his father. All his life he'd known his dad and mom as pillars that solidly, stolidly, held up the roof of Tommy's world. Reliable, supportive, but not particularly remarkable people. To think of Otis now, suddenly, as a teenage boy who'd defended himself with this weapon ... That past became yet another world, a new dimension, of which Tommy had just become aware. Again, the pinch, the pain, of such a revelation.

Tommy Tester took the straight razor from his father's hand. When he did, he could see the man's thick fingers trembling.

"You're a grown man and I can't stop you from making your way," Otis said. "I wouldn't even want to. But you don't walk into that white man's house unarmed or unaware. Anything goes bad, you get out, and you get back to me."

Tommy Tester nodded but didn't speak. He simply couldn't right then.

"I don't care if you've got to spill blood to do it, but you get out of that house at the end of the job and you get back to me."

Otis meant to sound stern, determined, commanding, but Tommy realized he'd never before seen his father look so scared.

"You hear me?" Otis asked.

"Yes, sir," Tommy finally said.

They ate quietly, and when the food was done, they left the Victoria Society. Down a flight of stairs and back to Harlem. In three nights Tommy would visit Robert Suydam's mansion. He understood the journey now as travel to another universe. No wonder his father felt fear; his son was about go so far.

"Why'd you bring that razor with you tonight?" Tommy said. "I never knew you owned the thing."

"Told me you was taking me to that damn Victoria

Society," Otis said, almost laughing. "Thought I might need the strop if those Caribbeans got wild. But I think you and me was the most dangerous Negroes in the place!"

Tommy had one arm looped through his father's to help the old man walk. His other hand was in his slacks clutching the weapon.

"If you're going to play at that party," Otis Tester said as they ambled back uptown, "I've got one more song you should learn. It's old, but it's got something to it. You understand what I'm trying to tell you? The razor is one way I want to arm you. This song is the other. Your mother taught it to me. Conjure music. We'll practice for the next three days till you've got it."

"Yes, Pop," Tommy Tester said.

Late night in Harlem on a Friday and the streets more full than at rush hour. Tommy Tester cherished the closeness, to his father and to all the bodies on the sidewalks, in their cars, riding buses, perched on stoops. The traffic and human voices merged into a terrific buzzing that seemed to lift Tommy and Otis, a song that accompanied them—carried them—all the way home.

4

THREE DAYS HAD PASSED, and this was the third night, and Tommy Tester left the safety of Harlem. He rode the same route out to Flatbush as he'd done when he met Robert Suydam, but now the journey felt more threatening because the sun was down. If he'd stood out among the train riders in the early morning, he might as well have been carrying a star in one hand rather than his guitar case now. Throughout the train car people squinted at him. At four different times white men asked him exactly where he was going. These weren't offers to help him get there. If he didn't have an exact location—Robert Suydam's mansion on Martense Street—he believed he would've been thrown off the train. Or under it.

When he arrived at the station, he was trailed by three loud-talking young men. The loud talk concerned Tommy. Tommy tried his best not to listen to it because he knew they were trying to scare him. If he shouted back, turned to fight, that would be the end of the night, no money earned, just a trip to jail. The streets of Flatbush became less crowded, more residential, and the young men quickened their pace. Tommy wore his father's razor around his neck like an amulet, but even that wouldn't help against three men.

By the time Tommy reached the grove of trees surrounding Suydam's house, the three young men were near enough that Tommy felt them at his heels. One walked so close the toes of one foot repeatedly kicked at the back of Tommy's guitar case. Tommy saw the mansion now, two stories and dimly lit, glowing from within the trees. If he'd been alone, he would've found the sight frightening, but because of his escorts, Tommy ran toward it. He crossed onto Robert Suydam's property; if he made it to the door, he might be let in before the white boys landed any blows. He didn't understand he was running until he was out of breath.

When he looked back, the three young men no longer followed. They remained at the fence line of the property. Even stranger, they no longer watched him. Instead they watched the Suydam home. They cowered before it. Tommy finally saw that these boys were younger than him. Maybe fifteen or sixteen. Children. Studying the Suydam home with fear.

Relief played from Tommy's eyes to his heels. Tommy crouched, looking for a stone. He found one the size of a baseball and weighed it in his palm. He set down the guitar. He wanted to hit the biggest of the three young men. They still hadn't returned their gazes to him. It was as if the house had mesmerized them. No better moment than this to take aim. He made a wish that the rock take out one of their eyes.

Then the door of the mansion opened. Barely a squeak behind Tommy but enough to make all three boys literally hop. They bolted like kittens, wriggly and mewling. Behind Tommy there was a groan as someone stepped out the front door and onto the boards of the mansion's wraparound porch.

"If you blind one of them, the police will be called."

This wasn't said sternly, almost with amusement. Tommy Tester turned to find Robert Suydam coming down the steps, one hand out. Tommy gave him the rock and Robert Suydam weighed it in his hand as Tommy had done. Rather than throwing it back into the dirt he slipped the stone into the pocket of his coat. Now he looked at Tommy expectantly. The moment lingered. Suydam waited. Tommy took a full minute to remember the word he'd been instructed to use.

"Ashmodai," Tommy finally said quietly.

Robert Suydam nodded and turned and walked back up the porch steps. When he entered the mansion, he left the front door open for Tommy to follow.

5

THE CLOAK OF TREES around the mansion did a great deal to hide its age, its infirmity, but inside there was no cover. The floorboards were old and poorly maintained; they looked splintered and parched. When Tommy entered the home, the entryway was lit by a single electric lamp, and he found the same in all three rooms on the first floor. This caused the edges of each room to lie in shadows, and it became difficult for Tommy to really understand the dimensions of each space. As if the mansion's interior was larger than its exterior. The smell of age, meaning undifferentiated time, had settled throughout the home, a musty odor, as if the winds of the present never blew through here.

Robert Suydam led Tommy down the long first-floor hallway, and Tommy clutched the handle of his guitar case as if it were a guideline leading back to the front door, down the steps, out the yard, out of Flatbush, back onto the train, to Harlem, and by his father's side. While they walked, the old man almost trotting, Tommy felt his guitar case jiggling as it had when the white boys had

"No, sir," Tommy said. "Whatever you like." He opened the guitar case and took out the instrument.

He had, in fact, expected to be paid to play for one evening because that's exactly what the man promised three days earlier. But a wealthy man's reality is remade at will.

Suydam reached into a coat pocket and revealed a fold of bills so thick it choked down all of Tommy Tester's pride. Suydam set it on the windowsill, then grinned at Tommy. Tommy strummed and played as expected. The old man stared out the windows.

Mercifully, the man wanted to talk more than he wanted Tommy to play. Tommy had only four songs in his repertoire, after all, including the one his father recently taught him. After playing for nearly thirty minutes, Tommy's fingers and shoulders, the small of his back, all ached terribly. He slowed his playing, strummed lightly, until he simply hummed in the cavernous old library. Finally Suydam—who hadn't once looked away from the great windows—cleared his throat and spoke.

"And it is my belief that an awful lore is not yet dead," he said.

Suydam wasn't speaking to Tommy, just reciting something half remembered. But Tommy, slightly dazed from the strangeness of this engagement, still responded.

"I'm sorry, sir?" he asked, and instantly regretted it.

Robert Suydam turned away from the windows irritably and glared at Tommy as if he'd caught a burglar breaking into his home. Normally, when a white man gave Tommy this look, he had a series of useful defenses. Looking down at his feet abjectly often worked; a smile might sometimes do. Tommy tried the latter.

"Well, what could you be grinning at?" Suydam demanded.

A third option, considered in a panic, was to get his father's razor out and cut this old man's throat, take the money, and flee. But by now, well past eleven, Tommy couldn't imagine making it to the train station. A Negro walking through this white neighborhood at damn near midnight? He might as well be Satan strolling through Eden. And if they found him with that wad of money, well, he'd be fortunate if the police were called. They might only beat him, then take him to jail. Much worse would happen if he got snatched by a mob. No razor then. He was, in essence, trapped here until morning.

"I asked you something," Suydam said. "And when I speak I expect a response."

No good deflections left, so Tommy Tester raised his head and returned Suydam's gaze. Might as well try honesty.

"I'm confused," he said.

"Of course you are," Suydam said. "The veil of ignorance has been set over your face since birth. Shall I pull it free?"

Tommy pursed his lips, trying to decide his best response. So far honesty had worked. At least the old man wasn't glaring at him.

"It's your money," Tommy said.

Robert Suydam clapped. "Do you know why I hired you? Why I was drawn to you three days past? I could *see* you. And I don't mean this charade." Suydam extended one hand and gestured from Tommy's purposefully scuffed boots to his well-worn suit to his guitar. "I saw that you understood illusion. And that you, in your way, were casting a powerful spell. I admired it. I felt a kinship with you, I suppose. Because I, too, understand illusion."

Suydam rose from his chair, and faced the wall of tall windows. The old man tapped at one pane lightly. Because of all the lights inside the library, it was impossible to see outside into the night. The windows had turned into a sort of screen reflecting Tommy and Suydam and the expansive library. Suydam waved Tommy over, and as he walked closer Tommy thought he saw movement behind him. The reflected image of the library's double doors buckled twice, as if someone were in the hallway, trying to push them open. Tommy turned quickly, but the doors weren't moving now. Tommy couldn't make himself turn back to Suydam yet.

"Your people," Robert Suydam began. "Your people are forced to live in mazes of hybrid squalor. It's all sound and filth and spiritual putrescence."

If anything could pull Tommy Tester's attention from the door it would be this. He turned to Robert Suydam expecting to find the man sneering, but the man had one hand on his belly, patting it gently. He looked up and to the right, like a man trying to remember a speech.

"Policemen despair of order or reform and seek rather to erect barriers protecting the outside world from the contagion," he continued.

Tommy held the neck of the guitar tightly. "You talking about Harlem?"

The spell broke. "What?" Suydam said. "Oh damn you! Why did you interrupt?"

"I'm trying to understand what in the hell place you're talking about. It doesn't sound like anywhere I've ever lived."

No applause for honesty this time.

"Mind your tone," Suydam said. He covered the money with one hand. "You haven't been paid yet."

This motherfucker, Tommy Tester thought and took one step closer to the old man.

Even Robert Suydam, for all his authority, sensed a change in the room. For a moment he looked like a man who realized a meteorite was about to crash into his planet. He raised an open hand, a gesture of peace.

"Tomorrow night you'll be playing at my party," Suydam said. "And the guests will be men like you. Negroes from Harlem, Syrians and Spaniards from Red Hook, Chinese and Italians from Five Points, all of them will be here by my invitation. All of them will hear what I am now telling you."

Tommy's temper became cooled by his curiosity. A white man's home crowded with Negroes and Syrians and all the rest. Suydam might be the strangest job he'd stumbled into yet.

"So why do I get the preview?" Tommy asked.

"I needed to practice my words," Suydam said. "To see how they affect a man of the proper type. Also, I admit you were convenient," Suydam said. "I needed those police to give me some room. The time they spent with you was enough for me to slip away. Thank you for that."

"You knew you were being followed?"

"My family has doubts about my sanity—this is what they say. More likely they have doubts about my will, and to whom, exactly, I'll leave this home and all its contents. Which of them will inherit the land on which it all sits. But they don't see it that way. Nobody ever thinks of himself as a villain, does he? Even monsters hold high opinions of themselves.

"My family is convinced I'm in danger. They've made

the police believe the same. They hired that private detective, too, the brutish one. His name is Mr. Howard. Mr. Howard and Detective Malone are collecting proof of my mental inferiority. For my own good, of course!"

Tommy laughed. "Talking to a Negro on the street won't help you look sane."

Suydam took his hand off the money and turned toward the window fully. He leaned with both hands against the ledge. "I know that I am high born. I mean that my family's old wealth, and their bearing in history, should afford me all the comfort I need. But comfort can be a cage, you know. Certainly it can stunt the mind. Time spent with my family, with my old friends of means, began to feel like bathing in porridge, drowning in a child's meal.

"So I sought out others, entirely unlike myself, and when they spoke of secret wisdom, I listened. What men like myself would dismiss as superstition or, worse, pure evil, I learned to cherish. The more I read, the more I listened, the more sure I became that a great and secret show had been playing throughout my life, throughout all our lives, but the mass of us were too ignorant, or too frightened, to raise our eyes and watch. Because to watch would be to understand the play isn't being staged for us. To learn we simply do not matter to the players at all."

Now he touched the window, tapping it, and the reflection seemed—for an instant—to ripple, as if they were staring into a pool of water rather than panes of glass.

"There is a King who sleeps at the bottom of the ocean."

As Suydam said this—against all possibility—the windowpanes took on the color, and apparent depth, of the sea. It was as if Tommy Tester and Robert Suydam, standing in this room, in this mansion, in this city, were also peering down at distant waters elsewhere on the globe. The guitar fell out of Tommy's hand as the image appeared. The thump it made, the sour note that played once, these hardly registered. A rush of cold seemed to enter not only the room, but also Tommy's bones.

Suydam said, "The return of the Sleeping King would mean the end of your people's wretchedness. The end of all the wreck and squalor of a billion lives. When he rises, he wipes away the follies of mankind. And he is only one of many. They are the Great Old Ones. Their footfalls cause mountains to topple. One gaze strikes ten million bodies dead. But imagine the fortunes of those of us who were allowed to survive? The reward for those of us who helped the Sleeping King wake?"

Suydam tapped the window again and the ocean—truly Tommy was seeing a vast and distant sea in the windows—churned, heaved, and from its depths a shape, too massive to be real, stirred. Tommy's throat tightened. He didn't want to see this. He thought he might shatter the wall of windows with his own hands if that thing in the sea depths became visible, distinct.

But then the image shifted, the perspective rising, leaving the sea far below. They left the continents behind. Was it possible? They left the world. They rose into the night sky. It really seemed as if these two men in a house in Flatbush were now adrift in farthest space. Tommy Tester clutched at the windowsill for balance.

"From here you might understand," Robert Suydam said quietly.

But Tommy didn't understand, he only wanted desperately to be home. He let go of the windowsill, turned, and picked up his guitar, and he ran across the library. He ran toward the locked library doors. Robert Suydam shouted after him. Indecipherable words. Tommy barreled through the stacks of books on the floor, sent them flying. He wanted to be home with his father, damn the cost. If he'd stared out that window any longer, something terrible would have happened to his soul. For all his confidence about his hustle, he understood that Robert Suydam was playing with a more potent force. He reached the double doors of the library and he opened them.

And Malone, the police officer, stood in the hallway.

Malone with his service revolver pointed forward.

"What?" Tommy said. "What?"

Tommy clutched at the doorknob. In his other hand he held the guitar. He expected to die as soon as Malone pulled the trigger. Was this who'd been behind him when he first entered Suydam's home? Had Malone been the one kicking at his guitar?

But then Tommy realized something strange about Malone, or about Malone's surroundings. While Tommy stood in the library of Robert Suydam's home, Malone stood in what looked to be the lobby of an apartment building and most certainly not the hallway of Robert Suydam's estate. What the hell was going on? It was as if the two locations—mansion and tenement lobby—had been stitched together by a haphazard tailor, Tommy Tester and Detective Malone facing each other because of a bad splice in reality's fabric. And actually both men looked mystified. In a moment Robert Suydam—breathless—reached the library doors and threw them shut. Then he slapped Tommy Tester in the face.

"What did you see?" Suydam shouted. "Tell me!"

"I don't understand," Tommy said quietly.

"Was it Him?" Suydam yelled. He reached into the pocket of his coat, pulled out the stone he'd taken from Tommy. He raised it, intending to break open Tommy Tester's skull. "Did the King see you?"

"The cop," Tommy said, almost breathless. "The skinny one."

Suydam held the stone high for two moments more. "Malone?" Then he lowered the rock. "Only Malone," he said quietly to himself.

"I don't understand where I've ended up," Tommy said.

Suydam breathed deeply, swallowing. "We can't leave this room yet," he explained. "Not till morning."

If Tommy looked baffled, it's because he *was* baffled.

"If we tried to open that door again, the results would be even stranger than what you've just seen. And potentially more dangerous."

Tommy looked back at the doors. His forehead went cold. "Malone was standing in the hallway, but it wasn't your hallway out there."

"I believe you," Suydam said. "But believe me it could've been worse. You might've opened that door and encountered . . ."

Suydam moved himself in between Tommy and the doors and stayed there the rest of the night.

6

CHARLES THOMAS TESTER left Robert Suydam's home at seven the next morning. When the sun rose, when they could peek outside the windows and see the streets of Flatbush again, that's when Suydam said it was safe to open the library doors. Before then, all through the night, Suydam explained, his home had been *Outside*. The term, the idea, seemed commonplace to the old man, but Tester had a terrible time understanding. The mansion had been *Outside*? But of course it was. Where else could a mansion be? This hadn't been the old man's meaning, though. Finally Suydam described it this way:

"Imagine a strip of medical tape with the adhesive gum on one side. Then a tiny ball of cloth is dropped onto the center of that tape. My library is that ball of cloth in what we call *normal* time and space. It is affixed to one place, one plane. But then imagine crumpling the adhesive tape tight in your fist. That ball of cloth now touches not just one surface, but many. In this way my library travels beyond human perceptions, human limitations of space, and even time. Those are meaningless strictures on a cosmic scale. Tonight we traveled quite far, though it seemed to you we were always in Flatbush. We weren't. We went to the shadow-haunted *Outside*.

"One of the places we traveled was the threshold of the Sleeping King. His resting place at the bottom of the sea. We were so close that with some effort I might have reached out and touched his face, seen his great eyes open. But last night was not the proper time. Not quite. When you ran to the library doors and breached them, I feared my years of planning had failed because of one panicked Negro! But we enjoyed some luck instead. All you saw was the cadaverous detective. Malone."

There had been much more like this. For hours. Suydam rattling off names, or rather entities, as effortlessly as the preachers who crowded certain Harlem street corners. But Tommy focused on the idea of the blip of cloth lost inside the ball of medical tape. This concrete image made the impossible easier to grasp. Hadn't he seen an ocean through the windows? Hadn't he witnessed the planet from the vantage point of the stars? Hadn't Malone been on the other side of the double doors, looking desperate and bewildered?

Throughout the night Robert Suydam returned to this Sleeping King. Like the planet revolves around the sun. *The Sleeping King.* At some point Suydam called this being by another name, his true name, but Tommy

Tester could never recall it. Or perhaps his mind chose to forget.

When the sun rose, Robert Suydam concluded with one final piece of wisdom. He retrieved the stone from his pocket again. This time he pressed the rock into Tommy's palm.

"How much did this stone matter to you, to your existence, before you picked it up to use it on those boys who followed you? That's how little humanity's silly struggles matter to the Sleeping King. When he returns, all the petty human evils, such as the ones visited on your people, will be swept away by his mighty hand. Isn't that marvelous? And what will become of those of us who are left? The ones who helped him. Think of the rewards. I know you're a man who believes in such things, and you're smart enough to make sure they come to you."

Then Suydam handed over two hundred dollars and walked Tester out of his home. Tommy remained on the porch long after Robert Suydam shut the door. A bright morning in Flatbush, that's what Tommy saw, but he had a tough time walking down the steps, and down the tree-lined path, and out to the sidewalk. He kept expecting he'd set one foot off the porch and fall right into an ocean where the Sleeping King waited. And why couldn't this happen? That's what paralyzed him. If all the rest could be true, then why not so much else?

Finally, the feel of the rolled bills in his hands returned him to the porch. He looked down at the money and told himself this was enough. Two hundred dollars would support Tommy and Otis for almost half a year. Go back to Harlem now and never return. Robert Suydam would never find him, because he'd never told the old man where he lived. Whatever Suydam had planned meant less than nothing to him. Let the old man have his magic. Otis and Tommy would spend the night at the Victoria Society, talking and eating well. He would make it back to his father, as he promised. That was enough. Tommy squeezed the bills once more, then dropped the roll into the sound hole of his guitar. It fell with a gratifying thump. He slipped the guitar back into the case and one hand into his coat pocket. The stone Suydam had returned to him rested inside. Instead of dropping the rock back into the dirt, Tommy took it with him. Eventually he'd spend his money, but the stone would serve as a souvenir of the night he'd been *Outside*.

On the train back to Harlem, Tommy didn't notice anyone else, and if they noticed him, he was unaware. The conductor made no small talk this time. Maybe Tester cut an odd figure. A Negro in worn clothes with a guitar at his feet and his attention focused on a stone in his hand. He must have looked feebleminded, and thus unthreatening, and thus invisible.

7

HARLEM. ONLY AWAY FOR A NIGHT, but he'd missed the company. The bodies close to his on the street, boys running through traffic before the streetlights turned, on their way to school and daring each other to be bold. As he descended the stairs from the station, he smiled for the first time since he'd left Suydam's mansion.

Tommy walked toward home, but found himself so hungry he stopped first to eat at a counter on 141st Street. The strangest moment came when it was time to pay and he had to fish into his guitar for the bills. The counterwoman looked uninterested right up until the roll appeared, as thick as the middle of a Burmese python. Tommy liked the way she looked at him after he paid from that knot, even better when he put down a whole dollar for a tip. Could Robert Suydam really make a man like Tommy a prince in his new world? Wouldn't that be damn fine? By the time he left the shop, he'd changed his mind about returning to Suydam's place. The old man had been right. Tommy Tester did enjoy a good reward.

At ten in the morning he approached his block, sunlight kissing every face and facade. The streets weren't as
tranquil. He hadn't noticed the traffic when he'd left the
counter, but by now the streets clearly had a clog. The
roads became more flooded as he approached 144th. His
block looked positively underwater. Three police cruis-
ers—Ford Model T Tudor Sedans—were parked mid-
way down the block, a much bigger Police Emergency
Services Truck behind them.

Tester moved slowly. The sidewalks so dense with by-
standers that people filled every stoop, too. The only time
he'd ever seen Harlem this crowded was when the 369th
Regiment marched Manhattan in 1919 after returning
from the war.

Halfway down the block, the police had thrown up
a barricade. Cops stood in pairs keeping all the gawkers
back. By now Tommy saw they were blocking everyone
from entering a specific building. His building. Tommy
made it to the edge of the crowd, right up to the barricades, and waited.

Malone appeared at the building's front entrance. Mr.
Howard moved beside him. They came down the steps at
the same pace, with the same gait, and for a moment Mr.
Howard became Detective Malone's shadow. Two more
police, in uniform, came out seconds later and shook
hands with both men.

Then Malone looked up and found Tommy instantly, as if he'd been sensitive to Tester's scent. He pointed and the two patrolmen ran to the barricade. The first grabbed Tester's neck, just as Mr. Howard had done when they first met in Brooklyn, and the other patrolman grabbed another Negro who happened to be standing there. They led both men around the barricade, to Malone.

"Not that one," Malone said, pointing at the second man.

The patrolman looked slightly abashed but then routinely went through the other Negro's pockets. When nothing illegal was discovered, he pushed the man back toward the crowd. No words had been shared between the two. When the man reached the crowd again, he simply turned, like the others, to watch what they'd do to Charles Thomas Tester.

"Your father's dead," Malone said.

This was reported neither with relish nor with sympathy. In a way, Tester liked this best. No pretense of concern. *Your father is dead.* Outwardly Tester took the news with great calm. Inwardly he felt the sun close its distance from the earth; it came near enough to melt the great majority of Tommy's internal organs. A fire ran through his body, but he couldn't show it. He couldn't open his mouth to ask what happened to Otis, because he'd forgotten he had a mouth. He stood there as blank as a stone.

"Tell me my father's dead and I'm going to take a swing at you," Mr. Howard said. "But these people really don't have the same connections to each other as we do. That's been scientifically proven. They're like ants or bees." Mr. Howard waved one hand at the building beside them. "That's why they can live like this."

Tommy felt the weight of the stone in his pocket. *Your father is dead.* He only had to reach it, swiftly bring it out, and spill these white men's brains on the streets. *Your father is dead.* The certainty of his own demise moments afterward brought him no fear. *Your father is dead.* He would have done this right away, but he simply couldn't move.

Mr. Howard watched Tommy a moment longer, but when there was still no reaction, he spoke in a more matter-of-fact tone, as if addressing a grand jury.

"I approached the home at approximately seven this morning," Mr. Howard began. "After finding apartment 53 I knocked several times. After receiving no answer I checked the door and found it unlocked. I entered the apartment, clearing each room in order, until I reached the back bedroom. In that room a male Negro was discovered displaying a rifle. In fear for my life I used my revolver."

Tester couldn't understand how he remained upright.

Why wasn't he collapsing? For a moment he felt himself—his mind at least—slipping out of his skull. He wasn't here. He was *Outside*. Didn't even need to be in Suydam's library to make the trip.

Mr. Howard pointed at the building. "Because of the orientation of the apartment, the back bedroom faces an air shaft. This left the back room in darkness. After defending myself, it was discovered that the assailant had not been brandishing a rifle."

Malone, who'd been watching Tester steadily, offered. "It was a guitar."

Mr. Howard nodded. "In the dark, this was impossible to know, of course. Detective Malone was called to the scene. He'll be writing up the report exactly as I've explained."

Tester looked from one man to the other. Tester's voice finally returned to him. "But why were you here at all?" he asked. "Why did you come to my home?"

"Mr. Howard was hired to track down stolen merchandise," Malone said.

"My father never stole a thing in his life," Tester said.

"Not your father," Mr. Howard agreed. "But how about you?"

Malone's long face slackened, and he pawed through the pockets of his coat. Finally Malone retrieved a pad, a policeman's notebook, and flipped through a series of pages. Arcane symbols and indecipherable words were scrawled across each page of Malone's book. Tommy doubted Malone's notes had anything to do with police work. He thought of Robert Suydam's library, so full of esoteric learning. Malone's notebook might be a journal of the same unspeakable knowledge.

Finally Malone came to a largely empty page, a few numbers written across the top. He showed the page to Tommy. Tommy knew it instantly. Ma Att's address in Queens.

"I'm going to tell you what I think," Malone began. "You figured you'd found a loophole in the job you did for the old woman. You followed the exact wording of your contract. You figured this made it impossible for Ma Att to come after you. Because you hadn't broken the rules. But it's 1924, Mr. Tester, not the Middle Ages. Her sorcery couldn't get you, so she hired out for help. She employed Mr. Howard."

Now Mr. Howard patted at his coat. "As I moved to secure your father's rifle, I learned it was a guitar. I then discovered the page I needed, hidden right inside."

"Don't you understand why I kept the page from her?" Tester asked. "Don't you understand what she can do with that book?"

Mr. Howard laughed and looked at Malone. "Did this man just confess to a crime?"

Malone shook his head. "Let it alone," he said.

"You understand," Tester said, glancing at Malone's notebook. The detective flipped the cover shut, slid the pages back into his pocket.

"I understand you weren't home when Mr. Howard arrived," Malone said. "As a result, your father was left vulnerable."

"It's my fault, then?" Tommy asked. "Will you be putting that in your report, too?"

Mr. Howard's mouth opened slightly, an undisguised expression of surprise. "I hate the lippy ones," he said.

Malone meanwhile seemed nonplussed. "Want to tell me where you were last night?" Malone asked. "Or shall I guess?"

Charles Thomas Tester had a sudden flash, an image of his father, half asleep, looking up to find some white man at the doorway in the semidark. What did Otis Tester think at the moment? Was there time, at least, to picture his loving wife or the son who'd worshipped him? Was there time for a breath, an exclamation? Time for a prayer? Maybe better to imagine Otis never woke up. That made it easier on Tommy, at least.

"How many times did you shoot my father?" Tester asked.

"I felt in danger for my life," Mr. Howard said. "I emptied my revolver. Then I reloaded and did it again."

Tester's tongue felt too large for his mouth, and for the first time he thought he might cry, or cry out. He felt the weight of the stone in his coat pocket, heavier now, as if dragging him to the ground. His night with Robert Suydam returned to him, all of it, all at once. The breathless terror with which the old man spoke of the Sleeping King. A fear of cosmic indifference suddenly seemed comical, or downright naive. Tester looked back to Malone and Mr. Howard. Beyond them he saw the police forces at the barricades as they muscled the crowd of Negroes back; he saw the decaying facade of his tenement with new eyes; he saw the patrol cars parked in the middle of the road like three great black hounds waiting to pounce on all these gathered sheep. What was indifference compared to malice?

"Indifference would be such a relief," Tommy said.

8

CHARLES THOMAS TESTER found himself cast away. First Malone and Mr. Howard brushed him back from his building—he wouldn't be allowed inside the apartment until the coroner finished up, and the coroner hadn't arrived yet. Malone and Howard walked Tommy back to the crowd. The crowd parted around him, swallowed and digested him. In minutes he'd been expelled at the far end of his block. Surrounded by onlookers but undeniably alone. He walked without thinking, found himself in front of the Victoria Society. He went upstairs and the greeter, recognizing him now, let him pass.

Tommy walked to the dining room, half full with an early lunch crowd, sat at a table in one corner, far from the table where he'd eaten dinner with Otis just four days ago. Tester stared at the table as if Otis might suddenly sit down, Malone and Howard having played an awful joke. Eventually three men did sit at the table, so Tommy turned away.

In time Buckeye arrived. It seemed like luck, but really the Victoria Society's greeter called Buckeye in. A greeter being only as good as his memory, he'd remembered the name Tester used for entry. Before Buckeye sat with Tester, he checked in at other tables, took numbers from those who wanted to play, and paid off one heavyset man whose number hit yesterday. Then Buckeye sat and bought them both lunch—this time cooked by a woman from South Carolina—a plate of Gullah rice, fish head stew, and hush puppies. Buckeye ate, but Tommy couldn't look down at his plate.

Buckeye hadn't heard yet about what had happened to Otis, and Tommy had no desire to speak of it. Still, the news—the horror of it—felt as if it wanted to leap out of his throat, an unclean spirit wanting to make itself known. To prevent himself from talking about his father's murder, he spoke of Robert Suydam instead. Even the wildest detail seemed less fantastic than the idea that right then, only seven blocks away, his father's body lay in their apartment, shot through until dead.

Though Tommy told Buckeye everything, he kept returning to three words in particular: *the Sleeping King, the Sleeping King, the Sleeping King.* Finally he put food into his mouth, not because he felt hungry, but because he couldn't think of any other way to shut himself up. He must sound mad.

By this point Buckeye had stopped eating. He watched his boyhood friend quietly, narrowed his eyes.

"When I worked on the canal," Buckeye said. "You remember I told you I was there for a year? When I worked on that canal, we had boys from all over the world. All of us brought our stories with us. You know how people do. And no matter how hard you work, men always make time to tell their stories.

"Well, we had some boys from as far as Fiji and Rarotonga. Tahiti, too. I couldn't understand the boys from Tahiti. They spoke that French. But the Fiji boys, two brothers, I swear they said what you been saying. *The Sleeping King.* Yeah. Them Fiji boys said it more than once. But they had another name for him, too. I can't remember just now. Couldn't hardly pronounce it if I tried. 'The Sleeping King is dead but dreaming.' That's what they said. Now, what in the hell does that mean? Those weren't my favorite stories. I kept my distance from those boys. You not planning to fly out to Fiji, are you?"

Buckeye laughed but it was forced. How could his friend from Harlem come up with the same story as two brothers from Fiji? Especially when both died during the construction of the Panama Canal? How could such things be?

Tommy, if he'd been listening, might've laughed along, but he stood, took his guitar, and ran out the dining room. Just like that. His case slapped the food off two different tables and the men cursed Tommy's back as he fled the Victoria Society. Tommy made toward the elevated train that would take him from Harlem to Flatbush. Hours ago he'd considered never returning to Robert Suydam's mansion, but now where else could he go?

The party wouldn't start for eight more hours, so Tester paid his train fare and waited on the station platform. Fiji must be damn far from Harlem. He knew it was an island in some distant sea. Buckeye's story served as some last corroboration. The Sleeping King was real. *Dead but dreaming.* He took out his guitar because he needed to do something to distract his mind. He practiced the tune his father taught him four days ago. Four days ago his father had been alive to teach him this song! The one Irene taught Otis and Otis passed on to him. Conjure music, Otis called it. As he began, he felt his father and mother were much closer to him, right there with him, as real as the chords on his guitar. For the first time in Tommy's life, he didn't play for the money, didn't play so he could hustle. This was the first time in his life he ever played well.

"Don't you mind people grinning in your face," Tommy sang. "Don't mind people grinning in your face."

Few on the platform gave him their attention, another guitar man in Harlem being as unremarkable as the arc lights along the sidewalks.

"I said bear this in mind, a true friend is hard to find.

Don't you mind people grinning in your face."

Until the end of the work day, Tommy played on the platform. His fingers never tired, his voice never gave out. Early evening he boarded the train to Flatbush. Either he was humming to himself the whole way or the air itself hummed around him.

9

"SOME PEOPLE KNOW THINGS about the universe that nobody ought to know, and can do things that nobody ought to be able to do."

Robert Suydam said this at half past ten. The party had been going for hours, but Suydam had yet to gather the group's attention. Instead he'd welcomed Tester early, and then, an hour later, the guests arrived, men and women and some in-between, as varied a group as Suydam had promised. The party was held in the library. All his books had been cleared from the floor. In their place were banquet tables, high-backed chairs, serving carts with cut crystal bottles of liquor—not bootleg swill—and glasses to match. The room babbled with languages. English and Spanish, French and Arabic, Chinese and Hindi, Egyptian and Greek, patois and pidgin. But the only music came from Tester's guitar. Suydam set Tommy by the bank of tall windows. He played standing beside the great chair. He sang to himself and avoided the eyes of the other guests. Tester knew how to recognize a room full of roughnecks. This bunch qualified. Suydam had haunted waterfronts and back alleys to find this crew of cutthroats. The kind of place Tommy imagined the Victoria Society would be was what these criminals called home sweet home.

Tester played and played. It was the same tune he'd been singing since morning. He warped and rearranged it, sang the words for a time, then hummed along for a while, and returned to the words again.

"You know they'll grin in your face," Tester sang softly. "They'll jump you up and down. Just as soon as your back is turned, they'll be trying to crush you down."

His playing was interrupted only once. Robert Suydam came close and raised one hand to stop Tester's strumming. He leaned in until his mouth was an inch from the guitarist's ear.

"You're with me, then?" Suydam asked. "I want to ask you before I address them. If I am Caesar, you are Octavius."

Tester spoke, though his voice strained from all the singing, the words coming out a hoarse whisper. "To the end of this world," Tester said. "I'm with you."

Robert Suydam stepped back and watched Tester's face solemnly. Tester couldn't be sure what expression his own face held. Had he said the right thing? He spoke the truth; it would have to do. Finally Robert Suydam turned away, grinning to the crowd, and he slapped the top of the great chair forcefully. The men and women in the room became silent. When he sat in the great chair, the guests found places at the banquet tables. Suydam flicked his hand to send Tester away. No one allowed in the spotlight but him. Tommy wasn't sure where to go, so he walked to the far end of library and posted himself near the double doors. Then Robert Suydam leaned forward and spoke.

"Some people know things about the universe that nobody ought to know, and can do things that nobody ought to be able to do," he said. "I am one of those few. Let me show you."

Suydam turned to the tall windows. Night out now and the lights of the bright library turned the panes into a screen just as they had before. Tester watched the crowd of fifty gangsters. He wished to see their reactions as Suydam's magic played.

"Your people are forced to live in mazes of hybrid squalor," Suydam began. "But what if that could change?"

The image in the windows turned a deep green, the color of the sea as seen from the sky. So they were *Outside* now? Suydam could do it just that fast? Tester lifted his hands and played, hardly touching the strings, no singing. Suydam looked up and seemed pleased. He played the conjure music quietly. The crowd of rowdies never looked away from the windows, but the music and

Suydam's words worked together, an even stronger spell.

All the old man said three nights ago was repeated. The Sleeping King. The end of this current order, its civilization of subjugation. The end of man and all his follies. Extermination by indifference.

"When the Sleeping King awakes, he will reward us with dominion of this world. We will live in the shadow of his grace. And all your enemies will be crushed into dust. He will reward *us*!" the old man repeated, shouting now. "And your enemies will be crushed!"

They shouted back. They clapped each other on the shoulders. Founding fathers of a new nation, or even better, a world now theirs to administer and control.

"I will guide you in this new world!" Suydam called, standing and raising his hands. "And in me you will finally find a righteous ruler!"

They stamped and knocked over their chairs. They toasted Robert Suydam's reign.

But Tommy Tester couldn't celebrate such a thing. Maybe yesterday the promise of a reward in this new world could've tempted Tommy, but today such a thing seemed worthless. Destroy it all, then hand what was left over to Robert Suydam and these gathered goons? What would they do differently? Mankind didn't make messes; mankind was the mess. Exhaustion washed over Tommy and threatened to drown him. Thinking this way caused

Tester to play a series of sour keys.

Suydam noticed even if others didn't. He looked up at Tester sharply, but quickly his expression changed. His annoyance shifted to surprise as he saw Tester raise the expensive guitar and bring the body down against the floor. Shattered. Tester turned to the library's closed double doors. Suydam shouted. First a command, then a plea. *Not yet,* he called. *Not yet, you ape!* The old man ran toward Tester, but the rowdy guests got in his way. Robert Suydam watched as Charles Thomas Tester grabbed the two handles and pulled the doors open. Then, to Robert Suydam's horror, Tommy walked through them and shut the library doors behind him.

PART 2

MALONE

10

MALONE LEFT HARLEM QUICK. He wasn't returning to the Butler Street police station in Brooklyn, where he'd been detailed for the last six years, but out to Queens, with Mr. Howard, to return the stolen sheet of paper—was it actually paper?—the private detective had been hired to retrieve. The two men watched the Negro guitarist stumble off after being informed of his father's death, then Malone made a point of thanking the Harlem detectives who called him in one more time.

They'd reached out to Malone as soon as they took Mr. Howard's statement. It was possible Mr. Howard dropped Malone's name, and a handful of bills, to make this phone call happen, but Malone made sure not to ask. Malone arrived, and was shown all the courtesy of a fellow New York City detective. He vouched for Mr. Howard's character, though, in fact, he thought very little of it, and soon enough the four men sat in the Testers' kitchen sharing tales about Harlem crime versus Brooklyn crime. Mr. Howard relayed stories of his scrapes as a lawman down in Texas long ago. They had a good time.

In the back room the body of the old Negro remained facedown on the floor where he'd died. The man had been shot eleven times, propelled off his mattress and into a wall, but his old guitar hadn't been damaged at all. The only sign it even belonged at this crime scene was the blood that stained the neck of the instrument. As the four men sat in the kitchen, they agreed the guitar didn't need to be taken as evidence. Everything was settled as casually as that.

Now Malone and Mr. Howard made for the 143rd Street entrance. They found themselves on the same train platform where the Negro—son of the deceased—stood playing his guitar. Even Mr. Howard seemed troubled by the reappearance, so the two men waited at the southern end of the platform. The Negro guitarist never opened his eyes while he performed. Malone couldn't guess the man was headed back to Suydam's mansion for a party that night. If he'd known, he would've followed him, rather than take the trip out to Ma Att's home.

Malone and Mr. Howard never spoke on the train ride out to Queens, and on the walk, their conversation remained clipped. Neither liked the other. They worked together because both had been called in on the Suydam affair. Not that they were making much progress. Malone secretly felt a certain sympathy for Robert Suydam, and disgust for a family working so hard to manufacture some pretense for separating the old man from his wealth. If Suydam wanted to spend his money and time seeking the more orphic knowledge of the world, what business was it to them? Perhaps Malone felt special sympathy because he, too, had a certain sensitivity. Ever since childhood, he'd felt sure there was more to this world than what we touch or taste or see. His time as a detective made him surer of this. Hidden motivations, spectral meanings, a certain subset of crime always offered such things. Most of the time his job allowed him to see petty desperation and conniving, but on occasion he bore witness to clues in a greater mystery.

For instance, the enigma waiting behind the front door of a cottage in Flushing, Queens. As he and Mr. Howard approached the place, anxiety assaulted Detective Malone. He became rigid even as Mr. Howard seemed at ease. As they approached the front door of Ma Att's home, the air became muggy and charged. While Malone pulled at his collar and cleared his throat, Mr. Howard remained roundly ignorant. He seemed to be in a good mood, like an enormous dog, gleeful and wild. Mr. Howard reached the door and instead of knocking, he kicked. The door shook and Malone trembled, too. *Be careful there,* he wanted to warn, but Mr. Howard wasn't the sort to heed or heel.

As the sound of footsteps approached, Malone swept

a hand through his hair and touched at his collar. Mr. Howard simply kicked the door again. He turned back to Malone, shook his head when he saw Malone looking stricken. He pinched his lips as if he'd like to start kicking the sensitive detective. Then the door opened and an old woman stood at the threshold. Mr. Howard spoke quickly.

"You're not too fast on your feet," he said. "I was about to leave."

Malone nearly gasped. Was it Mr. Howard's tone, his words, or the glimpse of the woman who'd opened the doorway just enough? Since Malone stood farther back from the house than Mr. Howard, he saw her silhouette inside. At the doorway, a stooped, slim woman had appeared, her nose prominent, hair pulled back tightly. But behind that woman, Malone swore he saw—what? *More* of her. Some great bulk trailed behind her, off into the distance of the gloomy front hall. Nearly anyone else—ones not so sensitive, so attuned—would've dismissed this as a trick of the shadows, a bit of bent light. Insensitive minds always dispel true knowledge. But Malone couldn't ignore the sense of her length, of largeness, behind the figure of this woman at the door. Not a second presence, but the rest of hers. Malone brushed his hair back again if only to disguise the quivering of his right hand.

Meanwhile Mr. Howard talked to the woman in his standard aggravated tone. But as he spoke, the woman looked over Mr. Howard's shoulder. When Malone met her gaze, she grinned.

Mr. Howard reached into his coat and revealed the folded sheet of paper. Malone hadn't asked to see the page this entire time. Not when they met up in Harlem, not when they waited on the platform, not on the train, nor on the walk here. The words of the Negro guitarist remained with him. *Don't you understand why I kept that page from her? Don't you understand what she can do with that book?* What did the Negro know? This question made him join Mr. Howard on his trip. Curiosity had cursed him since youth.

The square of parchment paper came out of Mr. Howard's pocket, and as soon as sunlight touched it, a faint trace of smoke appeared in the air. Malone smelled it before he saw it. A charcoal scent. Ma Att reached out into the light for it. She had an impossibly thin arm, skin the color of desert sand. She grabbed for the sheet, but Mr. Howard—to Malone's shock—pulled it back.

"The United States is a country of commerce," Mr. Howard said. "Remember where you are."

In the darkness of the house, something enormous rose, then swayed like the tail of a venomous snake. But Ma Att—the face she showed them—only smiled. She gestured for Mr. Howard to check the mailbox, and there he found an envelope. The private detective looked back at Malone proudly. Malone suddenly expected Ma Att to grab the big man with her tail—could it be a tail?—and pull him inside. But that didn't happen. Instead, Mr. Howard took the envelope from the mailbox and opened the flap to spy the cash. Ma Att leaned forward, her head and shoulders leaning past the threshold. Her lips parted, gray teeth bared, as if to tear into Mr. Howard's neck.

"Your name," said Malone. "I know I've heard it before."

The woman, startled, looked at him and pulled back into the doorway. She reached out in a motion too quick for either man to track. She slipped the sheet of parchment paper from between Mr. Howard's fingers quick.

Mr. Howard turned to her, and in one motion, grabbed the handle of the revolver he wore on his shoulder. The envelope fell from his hand, and the money scattered across the front steps. A breeze carried some of the bills across the house's lawn. Mr. Howard scurried after the cash. Malone and Ma Att were alone at the threshold.

"It's an Egyptian name, isn't it?" Malone said. "From what I understood, the woman with that name lived in Karnak."

"Oh?" she said. "And how much do you think you truly understand?"

"Not enough," Malone admitted.

The old woman nodded as if pleased by his answer, the deference in it.

"What is that book?" he asked, so quietly he couldn't be sure he spoke aloud.

"The Supreme Alphabet," Ma Att said.

"Now you have every page," Malone said.

"Come inside my home," Ma Att cooed. "I'll show you all the things I can spell with a little spilled blood."

Malone shuffled backward to the sidewalk. He never turned away from Ma Att. He never blinked. She laughed once and slammed her door. He found Mr. Howard on his knees in the grass counting his money. Malone ran off—actually sprinted—back to Brooklyn, back to his precinct. Mr. Howard shouted something, but Malone didn't listen, couldn't hear over the sound of his own panicked breathing.

Malone never expected he'd return to Ma Att's home again, but he was wrong. He'd be back one more time, but by then it would be too late.

11

THE SUYDAM CASE came to a close, at least for those litigious relatives. A court date was set and Suydam appeared before the judge, acting as his own legal counsel. The lawyers of the extended family argued that Suydam had become erratic and senile, but Suydam explained he'd become engrossed in his education, the learning a man disdains in his twenties but yearns for in his sixties. There's no better student than one who's reached retirement age. The judge, a man in his sixties, found this suggestion flattering and true.

As secondary proof of Suydam's decline, the family's lawyers brought affidavits from ten of his neighbors in Flatbush proclaiming the odd hours, and odder characters, coming in and out of Suydam's mansion. One night, it was attested, he'd entertained a swarthy army in his home. But Suydam explained this away as well. His learning had been in the fields of religion and myth, and New York offered the rare bounty of citizens from fifty different nations—a hundred backward tribes—many recent arrivals to the United States. Who better to interview about the beliefs of their people? He wasn't a madman, but an amateur anthropologist. If he was too old to travel the world anymore, well, New York brought the world to him.

Malone attended the trial each day, and when Suydam explained his esoteric interests, he felt affection for the old man. In the entire courtroom, Malone felt sure, only Suydam contained a soul as sensitive as his own, as aware of the greater mysteries.

In the end, the judge admitted Suydam's actions, and his company, might give any member of discreet society pause, but that hardly constituted reason to have the man committed to a hospital or stripped of his means. Suydam won out the day, sent his family, and their lawyers, slinking. Mr. Howard had been in the courtroom to offer testimony, but once the case was decided, the family no longer needed him. He made plans to return to Texas. He and Malone shared no tearful good-byes. A handshake was all, and good riddance. Malone's superiors returned him to regular duties in Brooklyn, and it was this return to his usual routine that, oddly, brought Malone back into contact with Robert Suydam. It had to, with Malone's work on the illegal-immigrant beat.

The legal immigrants of Europe—German and English, Scottish and Italian, Jewish, French, Irish, Scandinavian—all were welcomed through the immigration center on Ellis Island. A number of Chinese were permitted through this channel as well. But what about the rest? Malone's beat in Brooklyn brought him through neighborhoods thick with Syrians and Persians, Africans, too. How did they arrive in Brooklyn in such hordes? There were other, less famous ports for such immigrants, of course, but there was also a third channel, the illegal routes known only to human smugglers. Malone was concerned with this third path. It was his job, in fact. His superiors had him on the illegal-immigrant beat before Suydam's case and returned him to it afterward. Of the police working at the Butler Street station—perhaps of all the cops in New York City—Malone might've been the sole one who didn't loathe the role. The Negro, Charles Thomas Tester, had been right when he spied Malone's notebook—all those symbols and sigils—and counted him as a seeker of secrets. What better place to unearth them than the foreigner-filled warrens of Red Hook?

So Malone returned to the neighborhood. He'd missed the place. He doubted there was another white man on earth who would ever think the same. Robert Suydam, perhaps. These people, their superstitions and lowly faiths, were the lead a higher mind might transmute into the pure gold of cosmogonic wisdom. When Malone strolled the streets of Red Hook, he often found himself the one white man in the whole neighborhood. They were used to him there, and in this way, he became invisible. They spoke freely around him, if not always to him, and Malone's notepad filled with their lore. The denizens knew he was an NYPD detective as well, which brought him protection on even the grimmest block.

He also ignored petty crime. He never rousted the boys smoking fragrant cigarettes; he expended no energy breaking up the rooms where bootleg liquor was sold; why would it matter to him if the men and women in those rooms risked blindness, or death, for inebriation? There were police squads keeping an eye on such activity. Raids came if a local political office was up for auction, and even then, after a few photos and the exchange of many dollars, the criminals were set free. In this way Red Hook ran efficiently, its crimes quarantined—this was all society demanded of such neighborhoods.

After a week back on patrol, Malone making conversation where he could, sitting quietly in diners, eavesdropping on adjacent booths, he heard one name repeated more and more often. Robert Suydam.

Soon enough, Robert Suydam became the sole topic of conversation in the diners of Red Hook, heard from the clusters of clove-scented young men on street corners. Even the women who leaned out tenement windows and spoke to each other across streets and alleyways were invoking the name. Within weeks it seemed as if all of Red Hook were speaking with one voice, repeating a single surname, chanting it.

Suydam. Suydam. Suydam.

12

MALONE TOOK THE INITIATIVE to travel out to Flat-bush. A pleasant morning for travel, and a short walk to the Suydam mansion. Malone entered the grounds and climbed the porch steps; he knocked for a time, but no one came. He traveled the perimeter of the home trying to spot a light, an open window, some sign of Suydam. But the mansion had an air of abandonment, a body after the loss of its soul.

Finally Malone found the windows of the great library. Though tall, Malone still had to stretch to peek in. The shelves of the library—every one—sat empty. Nothing in the room save a single great chair, turned so its back faced Malone. His arms strained, pulling himself higher onto the ledge. In the shadow of the chair, on the floor, he saw a pair of shoes. At least he thought he did. Someone sitting there. Or propped up? Malone grunted like some beast, at the exertion of holding himself up. His arms trembling, his back tight. A shadow or the heels of a man's shoes? He wanted to tap the glass, but he needed both hands to balance. Then the shoes shifted slightly, as if the person in the chair—was someone really there?—was bracing to stand up. Malone throat closed up. He strained but held on. Now the chair in the room jostled—he was sure of it. The body in the chair was rising. Malone threw his elbow on the ledge. How could Robert Suydam not have heard Malone at the window? What proof did he have that it was Robert Suydam at all? Malone heard a man's voice—or really more of a vibration—rippling through the thick panes of glass. Malone couldn't decipher the words but sensed a mounting rhythm. An incantation.

Then Detective Thomas F. Malone got grabbed.

One powerful grip on the back of Malone's coat. He fell from the window and back onto the grass. A pair of very young men in uniform stood over him. One officer kicked Malone in the ribs. The other squatted, brought a knee down on Malone's chest, thrust a hand through Malone's pockets. The officer found Malone's service revolver but, in the rush of discovery, didn't recognize it as such.

"Gun," he said to his partner. "What else you got?" he shouted at Malone.

The second officer kicked Malone again, barked about "robbery," "criminal trespass." Then the other officer with his knee on Malone's chest found Malone's detective badge. This changed the tone of conversation. For instance, a conversation actually began. As did apologies.

The two patrolmen helped Malone to his feet. The one who'd done the kicking continued to apologize. But Malone only demanded a boost. The pair looked confused, but the kicker did as instructed. He hoisted Malone. Malone peered into the library. Not only was the figure in the chair gone, but the chair had disappeared, too.

13

THE NEXT MORNING Malone returned to Red Hook, but now he found only silence. When he showed himself, the streets went mum. A curtain of silence fell between him and the residents. The young men on the corners huddled closer, opened their mouths only when it was their turn to inhale. The women hanging out their windows shut their lips when Malone passed. When he sat at a diner booth, the men, daylong regulars, paid their bills and fled. Seemed like all of Red Hook had been warned away from Malone. Was this because he'd snooped at Suydam's home?

This meant Malone had to do something he detested. He had to consult the other police who worked Red Hook. Malone liked being a policeman, but he felt himself quite distinct from almost all the other cops. He'd tried, in his first two years on the job, to make friends with the other men, but they cackled when he broached the subjects that mattered most to him. Some even tried to have him thrown off the force. Poets should be dreamers, cops should be rough. That kind of thinking. And so Malone had retreated into himself—a kind of shut-in's existence—even as he attended roll call meetings, and occasionally shared information with other officers for a case. But after the denizens of Red Hook so clearly turned on him, Malone made his way back to the Butler Street station. He found the officers on foot patrol. He had every expectation they'd make him suffer humiliations before sharing any Red Hook news, but, in fact, the pair he found at the station—starting a shift—had been looking for *him*.

They looked scared as they spoke with Malone.

Robert Suydam had taken over three tenement buildings on Parker Place, one of the blocks facing the squalid seafront. Had he bought the buildings? Malone asked. And even if so, how could he take ownership so quickly? The patrolmen had no answers, only more startling news to share. In a single night every tenant fled these three buildings, fled or was put out. In their place arrived Robert Suydam, and enough books to fill four libraries. An army came, too, perhaps fifty of the worst Red Hook ever knew. All this moving done without a single truck on the street. Overnight, every window of each building had been blocked with heavy curtains. The property had been overtaken by the local demigods of crime and debauchery. Something worse than the patrolmen ever experienced brewed at those premises. All in the service of

Mr. Robert Suydam.

Last, they added word of a second-in-command, Robert Suydam's sergeant, a Negro heretofore unknown in the crime logs of Brooklyn. He acted as Suydam's mouthpiece, giving orders when the old man wasn't around.

"Black Tom is what they all call him," one of the patrolmen said. "Everywhere he goes, he carries this blood-stained guitar."

Malone didn't realize he'd fainted until the patrolmen were helping him up.

14

MALONE LEFT THE PATROLMEN and went directly to the waterfront. He knew Parker Place, perched himself on a stoop at the corner. But Malone forgot he was no longer the tall, gaunt detective the denizens of Red Hook tolerated in their crowds. Word had been spread. As soon as he sat on the stoop, took out his notepad, the tenants of that building shut themselves inside. Boys on the nearby corners darted away. The locals evacuated in the time it took for him to take out his ink pen. Nothing could be more conspicuous around here than a lone white man perched on a stoop. He stood, but before he'd even reached the bottom of the stairs, the groan of a wooden door opening played on the emptied street. The Negro from Harlem appeared from one of Suydam's tenements. Malone leafed through his notepad. Charles Thomas Tester. That was the name.

Despite what the patrolmen said, he did not carry a bloodstained guitar now, and this relieved Malone more fully than he could explain.

"Mr. Suydam asked me to come greet you," the Negro

said. "Do you remember me?"

His demeanor, even his voice, was greatly changed from when they'd last met. The Negro spoke with open disdain and returned Malone's stare so directly that it was Malone who looked away.

"Your father," Malone said. "Have you buried him yet?"

"They wouldn't release the body," the Negro said. "Not until the investigation is completed."

"It must be cleared by now," Malone said. He looked down and realized he held the pen out like a weapon. He did not lower his hand.

"I stopped trying," the Negro said.

Malone began to speak, but the Negro talked over him.

"Mr. Suydam wants you, and the other members of the police, to know that he has moved to this neighborhood permanently. He won't be returning to Flatbush."

Now the Negro watched Malone with the glass-eyed interest of a cat stalking a bird. Malone looked back to his notebook to escape that gaze.

"As he's doing nothing illegal, he expects to be left alone," the Negro said.

"We'll decide when to leave him alone," Malone said coolly. "And we'll decide the same about you."

There were faces in every window, in every building,

on this block and the next, watching both men. Malone felt it important to assert his role, his position, for the benefit of the onlookers, if not himself.

"Charles Thomas Tester," Malone said. "That's your name. And you belong in Harlem, not Red Hook."

"They call me something else now," the Negro said. "And my birth name has no more power over me. It died with my daddy."

"Black Tom? You expect me to call you that?"

The Negro didn't respond. He simply watched Malone patiently.

"I don't want to see you here anymore," Malone said. "I'll let the foot patrols know that if you're found anywhere in Brooklyn, they're to pick you up. I can't promise you'll be in good health by the time they put you down again."

Black Tom looked up at the buildings on either side of the street.

"Mr. Suydam is in need of a book that can only be found in Queens," he said, ignoring the detective's threat. "I'm headed out there right now."

"I told you where you're allowed to be," Malone tried, but his voice faltered.

"You shouldn't be here when I get back," Black Tom said.

What happened next was inexplicable, difficult to

even remember. Black Tom did something; Malone heard something. A low tone suddenly played loudly, as if Black Tom had hummed a drone note inside Malone's skull. The detective's eyes lost focus. Malone became dizzy from the sound, and he lost his footing. He fell onto the nearby stoop as if he'd been slapped. His stomach seized; he was about to throw up. Then a tremendous breeze sent Malone's hat off his head. The hat tumbled down Parker Place as if trying to escape. When Malone's eyes finally focused, he was alone on the street. Black Tom had disappeared.

Malone tried to stand but couldn't. He had to lower his head between his knees and breathe slowly for a count of fifty. When he looked up again, a young woman hung out the third-floor window of the tenement across the street, watching Malone.

"What happened?" Malone shouted. He could stand now, think; he clutched his head, patted his body, checking if he'd been shot or stabbed. He hadn't. His service revolver remained in its shoulder holster, though the metal felt warmer than it should.

"What did you see?" Malone shouted at the young woman.

She answered, but Malone didn't understand the language. The young woman continued, shouting really, the words flowing faster but never becoming clear. Why hadn't he ever learned how to speak with these people? Malone ran from the block, sprinted back to the Butler Street station, stopping only to retrieve his hat. He commandeered a patrolman and a patrol car. Black Tom told him exactly where he was going. Taunted him with the knowledge. Back to Queens, for a special book.

15

When they reached Flushing, Malone leaned out the door of the Model T, one foot on the running board, even as the patrolman went top speed, forty-five miles per hour. Malone kept one hand on his hat so it wouldn't fly off, the other on the door so he wouldn't fly out.

But when they reached Ma Att's block, they found it impossible to continue farther in the patrol car. The streets and sidewalks were too crowded. The morning when they'd put up barricades on 144th Street, the hordes of Harlem had swarmed. Now, instead of black faces, he saw white faces, but the numbers were nearly the same.

The patrolman beeped, shouted for folks to move, but it was like yelling at snow to shovel itself. Malone jumped from the car, pushed into the crowd, men and women bunched so closely together they seemed to be working against him. Malone shouted—he was a detective!—but his voice had a desperate tone. And, worse, it didn't matter to the crowd. They acted as if under a spell. What held their gaze?

When he broke through the ring of gawkers, he had the urge to cover his eyes. Instead, he fell into a stupor exactly like the rest of the crowd.

"How?" he muttered.

Only a week ago he'd been at this address. He had met Ma Att at the threshold of her home. Mr. Howard had been on his knees counting his money. And now it seemed Ma Att was gone. Her entire cottage, too. The walls, the roof, the windows, the little mailbox that hung by the front door. Gone. The front lawn, too. All of it had been pulled up out of the ground like weeds. Nothing remained but the house's sewage and water pipes. They peeked out of the soil like a partially unearthed skeleton. The plot resembled an open grave.

"How?" Malone said again, but nothing more.

Malone scanned the area for debris. Perhaps the house exploded. No debris.

The cottage had disappeared.

Malone recovered and realized he was first officer on the scene. He turned to the crowd. What had they seen? he asked. No one replied. They remained mesmerized.

Malone shook a few people at the front of the crowd, but they couldn't explain what had happened to the house. Instead, each one related a series of sensations—dizziness, nausea, a strange low note playing inside their heads. Most had been in their homes, not out watching the old woman's place, when these sensations struck. What drew them out to the street were one woman's screams.

"Which woman?" Malone asked, but none could identify her now.

More police arrived, as well as the fire department, and the crowd was dispersed. As people wandered, one woman approached Malone. It had been her who screamed. She saw the whole event.

"A Negro walked into the house," she said. "I watched him from my window there." She pointed across the street. "I was concerned because we have two children. I want them to be safe."

"Of course you do," Malone offered. "It's only right."

The woman nodded. "He walked right up to the house, and the old woman let him in. That was surprising to me. You see, she's never been too sociable. Not with anyone around here. But she let *that* sort in? My girl started crying in the kitchen, but I couldn't stop watching. I was so curious."

She caught herself, looked to Malone again.

"No answer you give will seem strange to me," he said.

She looked to the empty plot.

"That Negro came back out of the house with something in his hand. He tucked it into his coat, then he walked back to the sidewalk, looked at the house, just watching it. Maybe he wasn't just watching—I saw him from behind. Then the front door opened, I mean, all the way, and that old woman was right there and she was shouting at the man! She came right out onto the front steps, and I actually stepped back from the curtain myself. I had never seen that woman, not for a second, outside her home. Isn't that strange? But it's true. She had everything delivered, for years. Then she's outside. She must've been angry. That's what I thought. She came down the stairs to put that Negro straight!

"Now, I don't know how else to put this next part, so I'm going to say it like I saw it. Right? She stepped outside, and the Negro stood there patient as you please, and then it was like a door opened. You see, right there where the funeral home gate touches her property? Something *opened* right there. I say a door, but I don't mean a real door. Like a hole, or a pocket, and inside that pocket it was empty, black. I don't know how else to say it. Like the sky at night, but without any stars. And the whole time, my Elizabeth is crying in the kitchen."

The woman dropped her head, closed her eyes, and held one hand over them.

"Then that nigger, he just . . ." Here she looked at the plot of land, extended her left arm. She swept her hand, a brushing gesture. "He goes like that, like someone shooing a cat out of the house. Or when I open the back door of the kitchen, and I use the broom to sweep dirt outside."

"*Outside?*" Malone repeated. His lips felt dry.

"And then I couldn't keep my eyes focused, and I felt quite sick. I heard this sound deep behind my eyes. I'd been letting my daughter cry on and on. Now, why would I do that? I'm not that kind of person. Then, when I could focus again, I mean without being dizzy, I see that man on the sidewalk, but he's alone now. I mean the house is gone, and the grass is gone, and that old woman. Gone."

"And the door?" Malone said. "The hole you saw?"

Now she held her chin, looked to the spot. "I guess it was gone, too. I wasn't thinking straight. I ran outside. Can you believe it? I was going to catch that Negro myself if I had to. But by the time I opened my front door, he'd gone. I stood in the street screaming. It was that or I thought my head would burst with what I saw."

Black Tom had the book. Which meant Robert Suydam would soon have the book. Even worse, Black Tom had done away with Ma Att, somehow, with the sweep of his hand. If a mere lieutenant could wield that much power, what havoc could Suydam cause? Malone felt suddenly, entirely, small.

"And your daughter?" Malone asked. "Was she all right?"

The woman grinned, shook her head. "Cried herself to sleep right there on the kitchen floor. She'd been trying to reach the jar of peppermints."

Malone returned to the patrol car. He waved the patrolman over, and the two of them drove back to the Butler Street station. Malone spoke of what happened at Ma Att's home in vague terms. Property damage. Missing persons. Grand theft. He said nothing of what the woman had witnessed. His superiors would've spent hours interrogating the statement, disbelieving for days. And Malone felt sure they did not have days to waste.

Already Black Tom had likely brought the book to his master. Malone must scheme a way to get the entire New York City police force over to Red Hook with him. He went to his superiors. Malone claimed Suydam and Black Tom were bootlegging in the basements of the three tenement apartments and housing illegal immigrants from the most unwanted of nations. Finally, he added, the Negro likely kidnapped the old woman and dragged her back to a dusky tenement basement to commit crimes of a degraded nature. Malone's bosses were duly motivated. Within the hour, the concentrated forces of three different stations were gathering, an army off to battle.

16

THE PRACTICAL REALITY OF moving nearly seventy-five police officers, and the equipment needed for a full-force raid, meant squadrons didn't arrive in Red Hook until evening. By then there were reports that three children had been kidnapped and were being held in the tenement buildings overtaken by Robert Suydam. The children were reported as "blue-eyed Norwegians." Mobs were said to be forming among the Norwegians, in the neighborhoods closer to Gowanus, and the police needed to reach Parker Place first. Ethnic wars would become a problem if they spilled out of Red Hook.

When the force arrived, they cut off access to the street. Three Model Ts parked at angles at either end of the block, just as had been done on 144th Street in Harlem. Two Emergency Services Trucks were parked in front of Suydam's tenements. The residents in the adjoining buildings needed no warnings, no pleas to leave. They evacuated before the police had pulled their parking brakes. These residents gathered on the other ends of the patrol cars, lining the stoops of the homes on the next blocks. All of Red Hook attended this event. Locals climbed to the roofs of their buildings, or leaned out their windows to bear witness. They all saw what the police were unloading from the Emergency Services Trucks.

Theodore Roosevelt became president of the Board of Police Commissioners in 1895, and, though serving for only two years, he begun the process of modernizing the force. As a result, the officers had a bevy of weapons as they prepared to take the three tenements. Each man wore his department-issue revolver, but now, from the rear of the emergency trucks, an arsenal appeared. M1903 Springfield rifles; M1911 Browning Hi Power pistols for those who wanted to go in with a gun in each hand. Three Browning Model 1921 heavy machine guns were set up on the street. Each required three men to take it down from the trucks. They were set in a row; each one's long barrel faced the front stoop of a tenement. They looked like a trio of cannons, better for a ground war than breaching the front doors of a building.

When the 1921s were set down, they were so heavy chips of tarmac were thrown in the air. At the sight of the heavy machine guns the whole neighborhood gasped as one. These guns were designed to shoot airplanes out of the sky. Much of the local population had fled countries under siege, in the midst of war, and had not expected to find such artillery used against citizens of the United States.

The 1921s gave Malone pause, but what could he do? He'd called the forces in, and now they were loosed. He took his place and waited for the call to charge. The order came quick.

Malone watched the first wave of officers storm the tenement entrances. The windows of each building, on every floor, remained shaded and dark. Officers entered each building shouting, hoping to cause terror and surprise. In moments, the sounds of interior doors cracking open could be heard. The neighborhood watched the police work. Some looked curious, others sorrowful, but many were excited. The young men, in particular, thrilled at the violence. Boys cheered as the officers tore through the apartments, though the only side they were on was chaos.

Soon the sun set, and then it was night.

Malone finally took the stairs of the leftmost tenement. The one he'd seen Black Tom exit from that morning. While other police searched for illegal immigrants and kidnapped white babies, Malone went to find Robert Suydam. Up the stoop and into the lobby went the detective.

He watched as officers ascended to the higher floors of this tenement, while others milled in the lobby applying handcuffs to sundry, swarthy men who were being cleared from each apartment above. But it instantly struck Malone as strange when not an officer here opened, or even noticed, a door in the far corner of the lobby. It was as if they couldn't see it there.

Malone approached the door, and upon inspection he could trace, faintly, a letter written on the door. An *O*. The letter appeared to be little more than dust, but when he tried to wipe it away, the shape refused removal. Even when he scraped with his thumbnail to try breaking the circle, the *O* was not to be disturbed.

"Cipher," he said quietly. "Fifteenth letter of the Supreme Alphabet."

Malone looked to the other cops, but their backs were turned to him. They didn't even understand they had done it, the letter working as a sigil, influencing them to turn away. They reloaded their weapons, called up to the men on the upper floors, held fast to their prisoners. Malone could've shouted to them, but they wouldn't hear him. If Malone hadn't spent his life in study of such things, it was likely he wouldn't have seen the sign, either.

Malone tried the door. It wasn't locked. Why would it be? No one but Malone could detect it. Feeling anxious, he pulled out his revolver. When he opened the door, he nearly shrieked with shock. Black Tom stood on the other side of the door, but behind the Negro, it was Robert Suydam's home. Though Malone had only seen the library from the outside, through the grand windows, he recognized the walls with inset shelving. When he'd peeked this morning, those shelves were empty, but now they were quite full. Black Tom returned Malone's amazed gaze. He looked immeasurably younger, or more innocent, there in the doorway. He held a guitar in one hand, not bloodstained. Malone felt so overwhelmed that by instinct he began to pull his trigger. But before he fired, Robert Suydam ran into view and slammed the door shut from within.

Malone took his finger off the trigger, then looked back to the other cops in the lobby. Even this hadn't stirred their interest. Powerful magic at play. He grabbed the handle of the door once again. He stepped to the side so he couldn't be directly in the path if something strange greeted him again. But this time he found only a dark stairwell, leading down into the basement. Malone slipped his revolver back into his holster. He entered, and a rush of heated air came at him like a great beast's breath. The stench of river water made his face burn. He stood at the top of the basement stairs and squeezed the door handle. Turn around and get out—that was all he had to do.

"Don't hide your eyes now," Robert Suydam called from the basement. "If you are indeed a seeker, then come find true sight."

These words played at Malone like a taunt, and he closed the door behind him.

When he touched the bottom stair, Malone reached inside his coat. One pocket held his revolver, the other his notebook of arcane learning. Malone wasn't sure which he'd meant to retrieve. Which offered greater protection in this space. He chose the notebook this time.

This tenement's basement had been expanded. Walls torn through from this building to the next. Rubble remained in piles on the ground, half a dozen sledgehammers in a corner. The basements of all three tenements had been broken through so now they formed a single grand space. Kerosene lamps stood on the ground at intervals, offering Malone a dim impression of the great room. Hadn't Suydam and his people moved in not even two days ago? This was the work of many men, over many months. The magnitude of the labor alone made him shudder.

He did see one item he recognized. A great chair sat at the farthest end of the basement chamber. Not twelve hours ago that chair had been in the library of Robert Suydam's mansion. The chair was turned so its back faced Malone, and even from this distance he could see it was elevated somehow, maybe on a mound of dirt, so it resembled a high altar. The basement became a twisted tabernacle, church of a corrupted god.

In the middle distance a shape moved out of the shadows. A man. The detective hadn't seen this man since his appearances in court, and now here he was, hands in the pockets of the same waistcoat he'd worn to argue his mental capacities.

"Robert Suydam," Malone said.

He gazed at Malone, but in the semidark, his expression remained unreadable. Then Suydam turned, speaking to someone still hidden in the shadows. Finally Suydam raised his hand, beckoning Malone closer.

Even now Malone had the chance to escape, but he spied words written on the basement wall nearest him, painted, as if with a broad brush, in black paint. The paint dripped so only some of the words remained legible. Malone found his pen, opened his notebook, and transcribed what he could.

Gorgo, Mormo, thousand-faced moon.

There was much more, but in this poor light Malone couldn't read it all.

"I can explain, if you like," Robert Suydam said. He'd moved closer—so quietly—stood close enough to touch Malone's arm, or cut his throat. The smell of river water came strongly, the soiled odor of muck. Malone looked down to see if the basement had flooded at some point, but the ground remained dry. Suydam himself carried the scent. Not on his clothes, but from within. The old man breathed, and a wave of river rot reached Malone.

From here Malone could make out Robert Suydam's features more clearly, in particular his eyes, which bore a weakened light, as if the man had aged a hundred years since Malone watched him stand before that judge. Suydam reached for Malone's arm, but the touch was strange. Instead of holding Malone tight, Suydam almost shoved the man away.

"I'm all done in there, sir."

Black Tom. He stepped out from the middle distance, holding a bucket in one hand and in the other a horsehair brush. The brush dripped with dark paint.

"I've done it as you ordered," Black Tom said. "Spelled out a welcome."

Suydam let go of Malone and turned to Black Tom. "None of this could have been done without you," he said.

"I only serve," Black Tom said quietly.

The smell of the bucket reached Malone, an overpowering odor of wet metal. The bucket was filled with blood. The words on the walls painted with it. This is the moment when Detective Malone might've found the revolver in his pocket and killed both these men. Not a soul would've blamed him. But he didn't do that. Why not?

Robert Suydam grinned. "You want to see what more

there is."

Malone nodded once, almost ashamed. "Yes, I do."

Robert Suydam sighed. "It is the way of men like us. We must know, even if it dooms us."

Then he turned and bumped into Black Tom, who'd been hovering close behind. Black Tom dropped the bucket; it clanged when it landed. The remaining blood splashed out, leaving a stain across the basement floor. The empty bucket rolled over twice. Black Tom ran after it. In that moment Robert Suydam grasped Malone again, at the elbow.

Black Tom squatted, the horsehair brush still in one hand. He turned the bucket over. "It's all gone, sir," Black Tom said.

"Oh yes?" Suydam answered, and his voice broke.

"But I was nearly finished anyway," Black Tom said, then added, "sir."

Suydam let go of Malone and dropped his head. "Then I suppose it doesn't matter."

"I suppose not," Black Tom agreed. "No, sir."

Suydam raised one hand, gesturing for Black Tom to step aside. Malone and the old man walked together, farther along the basement. More words on the walls. Malone read some of them aloud.

"Justice. Queen. Born. Self. "

Now Suydam spoke the two next words. "Wisdom.

Unknown."

"The Supreme Alphabet," Malone said.

"Almost," Suydam answered. "One last letter is all that's left. And then . . ."

The old man's voice sounded weary where Malone would've expected him to be rapturous. From the street—as if from a distance of miles—Malone heard the shouts of his officers, then the unmistakable reports of gunfire. Pistols first, and then rifles.

"It's beginning, sir," Black Tom said. His voice, in contrast to his master's, rippled with glee.

Malone watched Black Tom. When he turned his gaze back to Robert Suydam the old man stared at the detective balefully. The sounds of gunfire on the street escalated, onlookers howled and screamed.

"You should see the rest before all this is over," Black Tom said. "Go over by that chair."

Then Black Tom pushed Malone toward the great chair at the far end of the great room. Malone didn't argue, or take offense; he moved forward eagerly.

Malone moved toward the great chair. His legs became stiffer, his feet heavier, and his mind swam as if through a murky pool. Was this merely fear and curiosity, or had the atmosphere actually changed as he moved farther through the room? Behind him Robert Suydam spoke, but the words were difficult for Malone to hear.

The Sleeping King!

Was that what Robert Suydam had shouted?

From the street, the sounds of heavy machine guns shredded the air. Not one, not two, but all three 1921s, all at once. Malone couldn't be sure he'd heard anyone shooting from within the tenements, but why else would the police open fire? How long would these tenement buildings stand up to a trio of antiaircraft guns? A cataclysm was happening on Parker Place, and belowground the air here smelled of sewage and smoke and the threat of divination.

"He waits *Outside*," Robert Suydam shouted. "Not a distance of miles, but dimensions. The Sleeping King rests on the other side of the door. He will be roused by a man of unwavering intent."

"I suppose that's you!" Malone shouted as he approached the chair.

A figure sat in it.

Suddenly a great wind picked up in the basement. As if a window had been thrown open during a hurricane. Malone reached the chair and grabbed at it to steady himself. A figure in the chair, for sure. Someone big. Was this the Sleeping King?

The room filled with a flickering light, and Malone turned to face the source. When it flashed, every corner of the chamber became visible, every shadow dispelled.

Malone looked back to see Robert Suydam and his servant Black Tom in the middle of the basement. And behind *them*? A pocket opened. A door. He no longer saw the basement stairs leading up to sidewalk level. There was, instead, a great bubble of darkness that was not pure darkness. Through this door he peered into the depths of a fathomless sea. And in that sea, the outline of something enormous, impossible to reconcile with his rational mind.

"I tried to warn you!" Robert Suydam shouted. "This plotting pirate means murder! The Black Pharaoh is here!"

The heavy machine-gun fire continued on street level, a thousand rounds, maybe more. The ceiling of the basement fragmented; dust fell. The police were tearing the building down with their Browning 1921s. Not enough to arrest the men inside, the tenements themselves were being razed. Malone clung to the great chair as though it was a dinghy in a storm-tossed sea. The seated figure, still in shadows, troubled him less than what he saw next.

Black Tom raised a hand in the air, and something silver caught the light. He pulled a razor across Robert Suydam's neck. Black Tom cut the old man's throat. Suydam collapsed, screaming. Malone hadn't realized a man could scream with his throat slit, but now he knew it was possible. Behind this murderous scene, the great door continued to open, the deep hole in existence expanded.

Malone moved around the side of the great chair. He dropped his notepad and fumbled for his revolver. He went down on a knee and looked at the profile of the figure in the chair. He knew this man. He almost choked on his words.

"Mr. Howard," he whispered.

The private detective sat in the great chair; even in death he wore an expression of anguish. The top of Mr. Howard's head had been torn off. Mr. Howard had been scalped; the skin near the top had curled and slipped. Malone shivered at the gray horror of exposed skull.

Malone's hand found the revolver in its shoulder holster.

Black Tom stood over Robert Suydam. The razor was still in his right hand, but he raised the left where he clutched the item Malone had taken for a horsehair brush.

"I had to be resourceful!" Black Tom shouted. "Mr. Howard proved quite useful when it came time to paint. At least a part of him did."

Malone steadied himself and gave a quick pat to Mr. Howard's knee. A death like this was not deserved by any man.

Malone rose to his feet. Black Tom moved closer to the great chair. Malone willed his hand to bring out the pistol. Above their heads plaster crumbled and fell. Robert Suydam, meanwhile, had yet to die; gone to his knees, stooped forward, clutching his cut throat as his essence spilled between his fingers, he howled in bewilderment more than pain.

"Even now he can't imagine he won't triumph," Black Tom said, gesturing to Suydam. The Negro held the razor loosely, a casual killer now. His fingers were slick with blood. He looked at the ceiling. "They'll bring this place down on top of both of you."

"Us," Malone said, hand still inside his coat. "Down on all three of us."

The portal remained open and, despite himself, some part of Malone reveled at the sight. His eyes adjusted. He was looking upon a city, lost to the ages, at the bottom of the sea. And in the midst of this decaying metropolis he saw a figure as large as a mountain range.

"Listen now," Black Tom said, pointing up at the ceiling, the maelstrom of gunfire and shouting on the street. "This is a song my mother and father never taught me. It's one all my own."

The heavy machine guns continued to rattle. How much more ammunition could they have left? The screams of the locals combined as if it were a single instrument, playing alongside the 1921s. And Robert Suydam, the poor devil, continued to live. He shrieked and his blood showered through his clutched hands. Each of these sounds were layered, one on top of the other, one with the other. A demented music, evil orchestration.

"It sounds as sweet as a ballad to me," Black Tom said.

"You killed the old woman," Malone said. "Ma Att."

"She can't be killed," Black Tom explained. "But she was dispatched."

"I'm an officer of the law. Don't you understand the consequences if you hurt me?"

"Guns and badges don't scare everyone," Black Tom said.

"How?" Malone asked. "How can you do all this?"

"Suydam showed me such things were possible. But the old man didn't have the character to see it through. I had to be the one to walk through the doors and greet destiny. Suydam proved to be like any other man. He wanted power, but the Sleeping King doesn't honor small requests."

"So why are *you* doing it?" Malone asked, sounding like a bewildered child. "If not for power, then what could be the point?"

Black Tom slapped one hand firmly on the back of Malone's neck. Malone had never felt John's Handshake. It was painful. Black Tom guided him away from the chair. As they moved, Black Tom kicked it over, and Mr. Howard's body splayed out onto the ground.

"I bear a hell within me," Black Tom growled. "And finding myself unsympathized with, wished to tear up the trees, spread havoc and destruction around me, and then to have sat down and enjoyed the ruin."

"You're a monster, then," Malone said.

"I was made one."

They moved toward Robert Suydam, who continued to gasp but had lost so much blood he'd fallen face-first to the floor. He gurgled like a drain. Black Tom marched Malone toward the portal, and Malone felt the sudden conviction Black Tom would throw him in, push him through. Malone feared drowning in that distant sea *less* than he did being any closer to that murky, doom-drenched, elder city and the being sprawled among its ruins.

"No," Malone whispered. "Don't send me there. Don't send me there."

"I thought you were a seeker," Black Tom said. "Well, here it is."

Black Tom forced Malone down to his knees. They were ten feet from the portal. The great wind that blew through smelled not of the ocean but of deep corruption. It howled and Malone's senses reeled, pummeled by a repulsive wisdom.

"Words and music," Black Tom said, speaking right into Malone's ear. "That's what's required for this song.

You can hear the music above you, but the words are not all done. One more letter needs writing, but I could use a little more blood. Would you like to help me with that?"

Through the portal, amid the ruins of the sunken city, Malone perceived the figure's enormous features—a face, or the perversion of one. The upper portions of its visage smooth like the dome of a man's skull, but below the eyes the face pulsed and curled, tentacles, tendrils. Eyelids the size of unfurled sails remained, blessedly, shut, but they quivered as if to open.

"No more!" Malone wailed, closing his eyes. "I don't want to see!"

Black Tom brought one arm around Malone's neck and squeezed tightly.

"My daddy's name was Otis Tester," Black Tom whispered. "My mother's name was Irene Tester. Let me sing you their favorite song."

Malone pulled at Black Tom's arm with one hand, but with the other he tried for his gun again. Even as Black Tom choked him, even as Black Tom sang, Malone kept one portion of his mind rational in the midst of so much madness.

Find the pistol.

Use the pistol.

"Don't you mind people grinning in your face," Black Tom sang softly.

Find the pistol.

Use the pistol.

"Don't you mind people grinning in your face."

Malone's hand found his coat pocket and slipped inside. He gripped the revolver.

"I said bear this in mind, a true friend is hard to find," Black Tom cooed.

Malone's hand came out with the gun. He had only to raise it and pull the trigger as many times as he could. From this close he would be deafened, perhaps permanent damage, but Black Tom would be defeated, and this mattered most.

Black Tom grunted. Suddenly he was doing something to Malone's face, but Malone couldn't understand what it could be. As Malone's hand rose, a new sensation crippled him. He'd been set on fire. So it felt. A burning pain whose cause he couldn't locate. He only knew it was an agony so bright the world seemed to flare around him. He howled as animals do, and the hand holding the pistol shot out against his will. The pistol fell from Malone's hand and flew through the portal, into that distant sea.

Malone screamed and screamed and let go of Black Tom's arm. He batted at his own face as if he might swat away his torment. Black Tom grunted again and Malone's eyes became wet. Something was being done to Malone's eyes. A tugging sensation, as if Malone's face was being yanked off. Black Tom held a straight razor in one hand, and it was slathered in blood.

Black Tom had cut off Malone's eyelids.

"Try to shut them now," Black Tom said. "You can't choose blindness when it suits you. Not anymore."

Through the portal Malone witnessed—against his wishes—the moment when a mountain turned to face him. Its eyelids opened. In the depths of the sea, a pair of eyes shone as bright as starlight. Malone wept.

Then the vision washed away. Malone's blood clouded his perspective. For the first time the firing of heavy machine guns was drowned out by new destruction. The middle tenement came down. This caused the other two to topple as well. Collapsed. To Malone the whole world sounded as if it had cracked in two.

Black Tom finally let go of Malone, and Malone fell to the basement floor. He whispered one last thing into the detective's ear. Robert Suydam lay five feet away, finally dead.

Malone made out the figure of Black Tom crouching beside him, dipping one finger into the detective's blood, then spelling something on the ground, directly before the portal. When Black Tom finished, the doorway closed.

The basement stairs, leading up to the street, became visible again. The door at the top of the stairs crashed open, and half a dozen police officers stumbled down. They thought they were escaping the worst by moving underground. But those officers must've thought they'd entered the bowels of the severest hell. They escaped a collapsing tenement building only to find an abattoir. The corpses of two white men, the tortured form of Brooklyn's own Detective Malone, the walls and floor smeared in blood, and one Negro standing tall in the middle of it all.

Two of the officers turned to run back up the stairs, but the collapsed mortar and brick above made this impossible. The other four immediately raised their guns—rifles and pistols—taking aim at Black Tom.

Black Tom walked toward them with his straight razor held above his head. Even in his pain and delirium, Malone shouted for the cops to fire. A cry of bloodlust. The last two officers joined their brothers back at the bottom of the stairs, and drew their service revolvers. Those six men fired fifty-seven rounds at Black Tom.

17

DETECTIVE THOMAS F. MALONE survived the horror at Red Hook and received the department's highest honors once released from the hospital six weeks later. He'd been trapped in the basement for twenty-nine hours while fellow officers, and members of the fire department, worked to dig out survivors. Malone was the only one to make it out alive. The list of the dead removed from the basement was Mr. Robert Suydam, Mr. Ervin Howard, and six patrolmen from the New York City Police Department. Every single body suggested death came at the blade of a sharp instrument, but no matter how closely the basement was inspected, such a weapon was never found.

While in the hospital, Malone was visited by, among others, the president of the Board of Police Commissioners, the chief of staff, and four different deputy commissioners. Mayor Hylan came to speak with Malone, as did Archbishop Patrick Joseph Hayes. A few members of the public wrote to Malone with questions that baffled the president of the Board of Police Commissioners; he vetted all such correspondence and sent none of it on to Malone. A man originally from Rhode Island but now living in Brooklyn with his wife proved so persistent a pair of officers was sent to the man's place to make clear he wasn't welcome in New York. Perhaps his constitution was better suited to Providence. The man left the city soon afterward, never to return.

Members of the press did all they could to infiltrate Malone's room, but the mayor had him in a private wing at New York Methodist Hospital for fear Malone might tell the press anything strange. It was feared he'd spin his outlandish story—clearly the result of horrific shock—but also they didn't want him photographed. The hideous image of a detective without eyelids would be the front-page story seen round the world.

The raid on Parker Place had generated positive write-ups thus far. Nearly fifty criminals apprehended, half of them illegal immigrants to this country. Those twenty-five would be shipped off, the other half incarcerated for an extended time. The collapse of the tenement buildings was attributed to a storehouse of explosives those criminals were stockpiling. Last, the three "blue-eyed Norwegian" babies were never discovered on the premises. Locals attributed the rumors of abduction to the swamp gas of European anxiety known to flare up within a neighborhood's proximity to Red Hook.

Malone healed as best he could and, with time, came to understand he must leave the police force. He couldn't imagine entering another building, another urban block, without collapsing to the ground, shivering with fear. His superiors couldn't imagine anyone ever trusting a police officer with such a vivid facial deformity.

The specialists at New York Methodist designed a set of goggles that Malone would have to wear for the rest of his life. He was given a solution with which to douse his eyes throughout the day lest they lose their moisture and he suffer pain and, potentially, blindness. The first pair of goggles was clear, but this only created a magnifying effect when Malone wore them. A second pair was fashioned out of darker glass, and this was deemed acceptable. It spared passersby the sight of a man who would never again be able to shut his eyes.

Just before Malone's release, a police surgeon who'd been called in to consult about Malone's eyes was ushered into the room. He told Malone about a town called Chepachet, in Rhode Island, where the surgeon had relatives—a quiet place, not urban, about as far as Malone could get from Red Hook but still enjoy the benefits of civilization. A specialist in nearby Woonsocket could meet with Malone, speak with him, as he continued his recovery. The NYPD would cover the costs of his stay, and it was implied this would become the place of his retirement. If he would disappear, New York City would pay the bills. Malone accepted the deal.

And yet, as always happens, the story did get out. What finally made the newspapers was a kind of mishmash of truths. A man named Robert Suydam became acquainted with the rougher elements of Red Hook, Brooklyn. The former member of highborn society, drawn into a culture of crime and terror, found himself corrupted by it, lost in a ring of human smuggling and child abduction. Suydam made his last stand in a tenement on Parker Place, and the police were left with no choice but to storm the building. After a firefight, the poorly constructed buildings collapsed, killing Suydam, one private detective, and six brave members of the New York City Police Department.

That, in its entirety, was the story that made its way into print. And eventually even Malone's memory changed. As he spent more time in the hamlet of Chepachet, as he met with the specialist in Woonsocket, Malone began to doubt his own memory of the villain known as Black Tom. Hadn't it really been Robert Suydam all along who'd guided those awful forces? Who else but a man born into wealth and education could be naturally equipped to lead? These were the questions posed by the specialist, and they helped Malone to reshape his understanding of what he'd endured. Who could blame

Malone's mind for wreaking havoc with the truth? Robert Suydam—that arch fiend—had killed Mr. Howard, and six officers, and brought grievous harm to Malone. But as a sign of God's just nature, Suydam's own Negro underling turned on him and cut his master's throat. Wasn't this, no matter how horrible, more likely to be the truth? Negroes simply weren't that devious, the specialist explained. Their simplicity was their gift, and their curse.

At the start of his time with the specialist, Malone would counter with the obvious question: *Where then was the body of the Negro in the rubble?* But the specialist waved such concerns away. Wasn't the site still being cleared, even two months later? Sooner or later the Negro would appear. And of course that was what Malone feared most.

"You are saved," the specialist said, during one session. "What has cast such a shadow upon you?"

"The Negro," Malone replied, but this was not a pleasing answer.

There was a story the specialist wanted, the same one told by the newspapers, and by every official with whom Malone had been in contact. Imagine a universe in which all the powers of the NYPD could not defeat a single Negro with a razor blade. Impossible. Impossible. And soon Malone was willing to be convinced. He began to half remember odd dream states, wherein he went down into the basement in Red Hook and found a portal to some hellish other world, and there he saw all manner of evil, but not a Sleeping King—*not* a Sleeping King. Robert Suydam was there in the dream, and there was a golden carved pedestal, and wild chaos ensued, and somehow Malone was spared. The specialist seemed pleased by this narrative, much more palatable; he assured officials in the NYPD and the mayor's office that Malone was making great progress.

Malone settled into his life in Chepachet and slowly rediscovered his interest in the arcane and profound. A handful of items had been shipped to him from the police department, the last effects from his desk at the Butler Street station and one item from the basement at Parker Place. His notepad. When Malone held the pad, it was like the first lightning kiss after a long time away from one's true love. Dust still coated the cover and the book smelled, faintly, of river water. Looking through the pages Malone felt some older, more certain, part of himself growing stronger. But then, on the very last page, he saw the words he'd scribbled that day in Red Hook. *Gorgo, Mormo, thousand-faced moon.* But this wasn't what made him falter. Instead it was a series of words transcribed in the order he'd read them. The Supreme Alphabet.

One more letter needs writing, but I could use a little

more blood.

Would you like to help me with that?

Malone squeezed the notepad tightly, an involuntary spasm, and he was transported back to Parker Place, his eyes bleeding and his face burning, and the Negro stooped over him. He whispered something in Malone's ear. Then he dipped his finger in blood and moved it on the ground. The Supreme Alphabet spelled out in gore. Malone could almost see the last letter, actually three short words, scrawled on the basement floor. The same words had been on the covers of the book Charles Thomas Tester brought to Ma Att long ago.

Even as he became nauseated from the memory, he found himself turning his head, inching his right ear forward, as if to hear the last words Black Tom ever spoke. What was it? Only one line. But there, in the little cabin in Rhode Island, where he'd made his new home, the words would not come to him.

Instead, the modest space began to crowd him as it had never done in the months he'd lived there. He feared the walls of the cabin would collapse and the roof would come down. Along the wall he saw the six officers, lined up as they'd been on the stairwell when they'd fired on Black Tom. The way they'd dropped their guns and clutched at their ears after the tremendous echo of their gunfire. And then Black Tom appeared at the top of the stairs—as if he'd just stepped in from outside—and moved down the line behind them, cutting each man's throat in turn, all too confused to realize they'd been murdered.

And right afterward, at the bottom of those steps, Black Tom made the strange but now familiar sound—a long, low tone—and a blast of fetid air coursed through the basement. He didn't even need the protection of Robert Suydam's library in order to move through time and dimension. He'd become a star traveler in no need of a ship. Then Black Tom, the former Charles Thomas Tester, walked through the portal. He went out.

All this returned to Malone there in the cabin, and he couldn't stay inside. He ran out but still felt unguarded. He walked down the Chepachet road, out of the hamlet, to the nearby village of Pascoag, slightly more urban with its tiny downtown, a handful of taller buildings. Malone told himself he'd come here to pick up some magazines, maybe eat lunch, but none of this was true. He felt himself hunted, hounded, but couldn't understand what might be following him. The stories he, and his specialist, had used to paper over the truth had suddenly been torn off.

Thomas J. Malone walked Sayles Avenue, and soon reached Main Street. He made a strange sight to passersby, this tall, anxious man wearing enormous shaded goggles. He became more alien when, on Main Street, he turned and faced the tallest building in all of downtown Pascoag. He looked up once and fell to the ground, screaming so hideously it made a horse drawing a carriage bolt forward; its driver had a terrible time getting the spooked animal to stop. Pedestrians gathered around the odd man, who looked up at the skies. They asked after him—a child was sent to fetch the local sheriff—but the man only gawped at the skyline, such as it was, and his mouth quivered as if he were about to bawl. What had happened? the crowd wondered aloud. What did he see? Many dismissed Malone as a drunk or a madman, but a handful—the more sensitive souls—followed his sightline. For a moment all of them glimpsed an abhorrent face in the looming clouds. Each one saw what Malone had seen, the thing that had brought him to the ground. A pair of inhuman eyes stared down at them from the heavens, shining like starlight. Then and there, Malone finally heard the last words Black Tom whispered down in the basement.

I'll take Cthulhu over you devils any day.

Then Malone returned to himself and, realizing he'd made a scene, he apologized to the gathered townspeople. After explaining himself to the local constable, he wandered back to his cabin in Chepachet and became, for a short while, an item of lively gossip in Pascoag.

18

BLACK TOM ENTERED THE Victoria Society and took a table in the dining room, one near the windows looking out on 137th Street. As soon as he arrived, he slipped the straight razor into his pocket and removed his jacket and vest. He'd cleaned up a little, but it hardly helped. His pants remained clotted with dirt and dark with blood, and his shirt showed so much perspiration that it clung to his skin. Still he was allowed entrance. The greeter feared him.

Black Tom sat in the dining room, and since it was late afternoon the space remained otherwise empty. He sat with his back to everything and watched the sun glow over Harlem, and he listened to the rumbling hive of life on the sidewalks and the streets.

When Buckeye arrived, a plate of food had been set before Black Tom. He hadn't eaten anything. Buckeye ordered his own plate—a meal made by a Puerto Rican woman this time—and didn't really look at Black Tom until he'd eaten two alcapurrias. The greeter had sent out word that Buckeye's friend was at the Victoria Society, looking decidedly *odd*.

"I heard about your father," Buckeye said after he'd swallowed.

"My father?" Black Tom said this as if he'd forgotten he ever had one.

"Where you been, man?" Buckeye asked, setting down his fork. "What happened to you?"

"You'll hear about it," Black Tom said calmly. "It'll be in the papers tomorrow. Probably for a whole week. Then they'll move on to something else."

Buckeye watched Black Tom quietly. He'd been hustling long enough to know there are questions you don't ask if you want to avoid being pulled into a court case later.

Black Tom said, "I did something big, bigger than anyone will understand for a long time. I was just so angry."

Buckeye nodded, ate another few bites of mofongo, and strenuously did *not* ask follow-up questions.

"I was a good man, right? I mean I wasn't like my father, but I never did people wrong. Not truly."

"No, you didn't," Buckeye said, looking his old friend directly in the eye. "You were always good people. Still are."

Black Tom smiled faintly but shook his head. "Every time I was around them, they acted like I was a monster.

So I said goddamnit, I'll be the worst monster you ever saw!"

Newly arrived diners at nearby tables turned to look at Black Tom, but neither he nor Buckeye noticed.

"But I forgot," Black Tom said quietly. "I forgot about all this."

Black Tom scanned the tables of men and women dining at the Victoria Society. He pointed to the row of windows that opened onto 137th Street.

"Nobody here ever called me a monster," Black Tom said. "So why'd I go running somewhere else, to be treated like a dog? Why couldn't I see all the good things I already had? Malone said I put my daddy at risk, and he was right. It's my fault, too. I used him without a second thought."

Black Tom reached into his pocket and revealed the straight razor. Buckeye gave a quick glance around the room, but Black Tom paid the room no mind. He opened the razor. The blade looked slathered in jelly. Buckeye knew what that was. Black Tom set the strop down on the table and Buckeye tossed his napkin over it.

"We need to get rid of that," Buckeye cautioned, looking at the shape under the napkin. "You should have done it before you even stepped in here."

"The seas will rise and our cities will be swallowed by the oceans," Black Tom said. "The air will grow so hot we won't be able to breathe. The world will be remade for Him, and His kind. That white man was afraid of indifference; well, now he's going to find out what it's like.

"I don't know how long it'll take. Our time and their time isn't counted the same. Maybe a month? Maybe a hundred years? All this will pass. Humanity will be washed away. The globe will be theirs again, and it's me who did it. Black Tom did it. I gave them the world."

"Who the fuck is Black Tom?" Buckeye asked.

"Me," he said.

Buckeye scanned the room once more, then grabbed the napkin and the razor blade as well. He folded the napkin around the blade.

"Your name is Tommy Tester," Buckeye said. "*Charles Thomas Tester.* You're my best friend, and the worst singer I've ever heard."

Both men laughed loudly, and for a brief moment Black Tom appeared as he had been not so long ago: twenty years old and in possession of great joy.

"I wish I'd been more like my father," Black Tom said. "He didn't have much, but he never lost his soul."

Buckeye had slid back from the table, fussed with his right boot, trying to slip the straight razor inside for safekeeping. He'd discard it, into the river, after he walked Tommy home.

"I wonder if I could ever get mine back," Black Tom

whispered.

He rose from the table and walked to a window. He opened it. At 4:13 p.m., Harlemites within a three-block radius reported a strange sound in their heads, and a sudden wave of nausea. Before anyone inside the Victoria Society realized what was happening, Black Tom went out the window. Buckeye turned in time to see him leap, but Tommy Tester's body was never found. Zig zag zig.

About the Author

Photograph by Emily Raboteau

VICTOR LAVALLE is the author of four books: *Slapboxing with Jesus, The Ecstatic, Big Machine,* and *The Devil in Silver.* He has been a recipient of numerous awards, including a Shirley Jackson Award and an American Book Award. He first learned of the Supreme Alphabet at the age of eighteen. He has been using it ever since.

TOR·COM

Science fiction. Fantasy. The universe.

And related subjects.

*

More than just a publisher's website, *Tor.com* is a venue for **original fiction, comics,** and **discussion** of the entire field of SF and fantasy, in all media and from all sources. Visit our site today—and join the conversation yourself.